"*Must you always be so offensive?*"

"Why, what do you mean, darlin'?" she taunted, realizing that was her only means of defense. She lifted her hand and let her knuckles slide down his cheek, which was roughened by a fine stubbling of silvery-blond beard. "I was only teasing, wasn't I? Everyone knows you're Daddy's blue-eyed boy!"

Cole's hand clamped about her wrist, dragging it down to his side. "You can't wait to cause trouble, can you?" he snarled, and although his grasp was painful, the burning frustration in his eyes wasn't.

"Careful, darlin'," she murmured, her slim fingers reaching out to stroke the taut muscle of his thigh, exposed by the tight-fitting denim. "Your mother might be watching and we wouldn't want her to think we can't get along."

ANNE MATHER began her career by writing the kind of book she likes to read—romance. Married, with two children, this author from the north of England has become a favorite with readers of romance fiction the world over. Since her first novel was published in 1970, Anne Mather has written more than eighty romances, with over ninety million copies sold!

Books by Anne Mather

STORMSPELL
WILD CONCERTO
HIDDEN IN THE FLAME
THE LONGEST PLEASURE

HARLEQUIN PRESENTS PLUS
1567—RICH AS SIN

HARLEQUIN PRESENTS
1444—BLIND PASSION
1458—SUCH SWEET POISON
1492—BETRAYED
1514—DIAMOND FIRE
1542—GUILTY
1553—DANGEROUS SANCTUARY

Anne Mather

Tidewater Seduction

Harlequin Books

TORONTO • NEW YORK • LONDON
AMSTERDAM • PARIS • SYDNEY • HAMBURG
STOCKHOLM • ATHENS • TOKYO • MILAN
MADRID • WARSAW • BUDAPEST • AUCKLAND

Harlequin Presents Plus first edition October 1993
ISBN 0-373-11591-1

Original hardcover edition published in 1992
by Mills & Boon Limited

TIDEWATER SEDUCTION

CHAPTER ONE

IT COULDN'T be him: it shouldn't be him; but it was. Striding towards her, across the terrace where she was having breakfast, giving every indication he had expected to find her there.

Joanna glanced, half guiltily, about her, wondering even then if she was making a mistake. Maybe he had seen someone else—some other guest. But no. She was breakfasting late, and the hotel coffee shop was almost empty, most of the other guests all too eager to acquire that all-important tan. She was the only person sitting in her corner of the terrace, her olive skin as brown now as it was ever going to get.

Uncle Charles, her father's brother, used to say, teasingly, that she was the changeling in their otherwise so-English family. With her dark skin and silky black hair, she was nothing like her blonde and brown-haired parents. She had to be a throw-back to some scandalous liaison in the family's history. But until her marriage to Cole Macallister she hadn't found it a problem. Of course, that marriage, and the much-publicised divorce that had followed, had rather shaken her confidence. But, in recent months, she had managed to put the past behind her. Until this moment, she acknowledged tensely, experiencing an almost overwhelming urge to run, kicking and screaming, from a confrontation she had never thought to have to face.

Happily, she succeeded in controlling that compulsion, however, and by the time he stopped beside her table she had even contrived a faintly ironic smile. What the hell! She had nothing to be ashamed of, she assured herself tautly, crossing one long leg over the other in an unconsciously defensive gesture. She had just as much right to be here as he had.

'Hello, Jo.'

His greeting was scarcely original, and she gained assurance from his diffidence. 'Cole,' she returned coolly, toying with the handle of her coffee-cup. 'How are you?'

'Fine.'

And he looked it, she conceded reluctantly. Even though he had never been a conventionally handsome man, the harsh planes and angles of his lean features possessed a much more potent attraction. A latent sexuality radiated from eyes as blue as amethysts, fringed by short thick lashes, several shades darker than his hair. There were rugged hollows beneath his arching cheekbones, and she knew his nose had been broken in his youth. But his mouth was what drew her gaze, thin, and hard, and masculine, yet infinitely sensual, and gentler than when she'd last seen it.

But the silvery blond hair was the same, she noticed, chiding the treacherous emotions that still found beauty in his face. Longer than was fashionable, it brushed the open collar of his chambray shirt, the fine strands upturned against his neck. He was not a man you could ever ignore, thought Joanna uneasily, though God knew she had done her best to do so for the past three years.

'May I join you?'

The question was unexpected, and for a moment Joanna knew the mouth-drying sense of panic she had experienced when she first saw him coming towards her. No, she wanted to say harshly. No, you can't. I don't want you to. I don't want to talk to you. I don't want you spoiling my affection for these islands by your presence.

But, of course, she didn't say any of those things. Although she knew she was probably being incredibly stupid, she was far too—polite—to behave so childishly, so *obviously*.

So, instead, 'Why not?' she murmured, moving her glass of orange juice aside, and relocating the cooling pot of coffee. 'Be my guest.'

'Thanks.'

With the inherent grace that had always seemed so unusual in a man of his size, Cole pulled out one of the vinyl-cushioned plastic chairs, and, turning its back to the table, straddled it. His bony knee, clad in cream cotton trousers, brushed the side of her bare thigh as he positioned himself, and it was all Joanna could do not to flinch away from even that slight contact. But Cole seemed not to notice any withdrawal on her part, as he draped his arms along the back of the chair, and cast a casual eye over the palm-shaded stretch of sand only a few yards away.

'Beautiful, isn't it?' he observed, and Joanna disciplined herself to make the obvious rejoinder.

'Beautiful,' she agreed, looking towards the ocean, creaming on to the crushed coral, beyond the coloured umbrellas, and oil-slick bodies. Although it wasn't the Caribbean, the waters cradling the sun-rich islands of the Bahamas were every bit as warm and inviting, their blue-green depths a magnet for yachtsmen and under-water explorers alike. 'I've always loved it.'

'Yes.' Cole's mouth compressed. 'Your family have a villa here, don't they?'

His brows, distinctly darker than the ash-pale sub-tlety of his hair, drew together speculatively, but be-fore he could voice the question his words had provoked Joanna forestalled him.

'Not any more,' she stated swiftly, avoiding his en-quiring gaze. 'In any case, it's not important. And I'm sure it has nothing to do with why you're here.'

'No.' Cole agreed with her. 'But you are.'

Joanna stared at him. 'You knew I was here?'

'Obviously.'

'No, not obviously.' She felt her nails digging into her palms, and determinedly relaxed herself. 'I as-sumed you must be here on holiday. That—that this meeting was accidental.'

'Hardly.' Cole regarded her dispassionately. 'That would be quite a coincidence, wouldn't it?'

Joanna took a steadying breath. 'Then I think you'd better leave. Or I will.'

She wanted to get to her feet. She wanted to walk away from the table, and pretend this had never hap-pened. Perhaps, if she pinched herself hard enough, she might wake up. Oh, what she would give to find out this was all a dream—or a nightmare!

But she had run away from Cole once before, and she was damned if she'd do it again. He couldn't hurt her now. Not any more. And she would just be play-ing into his hands, if she allowed him to see he had up-set her.

So, with admirable restraint, she helped herself to a croissant, from the napkin-lined basket in front of her, and picked up her knife to butter it.

Cole watched her. She was aware of his gaze, though she didn't acknowledge it. He had always had the ability to make her aware of him, even when she least wanted it. There was a brooding intensity to his appraisal that pierced any façade of indifference she might raise against him. Even now, buttering her croissant, with hands that only by a supreme effort on her part remained steady, she could feel his eyes upon her. What was he thinking? she wondered. What did he want? And how had he known where she was?

'Prickly, aren't you?' he said at last, and Joanna fought back the angry defence that sprang to her lips.

'I'm—curious,' she admitted, proud of the lack of aggression in her tone. 'How did you know I was here?'

'Grace told me,' he replied, mentioning his aunt's name without inflexion. 'You must know we keep in touch. And just because she's English, you shouldn't automatically assume she'll take your side.'

Joanna swallowed hard. Grace, she thought grimly. She should have guessed. Blood was thicker than water, and the Macallisters—even estranged ones—evidently believed that stronger than most.

'Don't think badly of her,' Cole said now, as Joanna stared down at the croissant. 'She didn't have a lot of choice. Not in the circumstances.'

But Joanna wasn't listening to him. Damn Grace, she was thinking, abandoning the untouched roll in favour of another cup of coffee. She knew, better than anyone, that for the past three years Joanna had done her utmost to forget Cole, and what he had done to her life. How could Grace have told him she was here, taking the first holiday she had had in twenty solid months of hard slog? This was supposed to be her reward to herself for finishing ahead of time. The paintings for the exhibition were completed. She hadn't even brought her materials with her. She had intended to have a complete break. And now——

'Where's—Sammy-Jean?' she demanded, looking beyond him, as if expecting the other woman to appear. 'You did marry her, didn't you?' She forced a mocking lilt into her voice, as she added, 'Sammy-Jean Macallister! Oh, yes, that sounds so much better than Joanna Macallister ever did.'

Cole's lips tightened. 'You won't get an argument from me,' he retorted, but she realised to her amazement—and delight—that, for once, she had got under his skin. A faint trace of colour ran up beneath his tan, and the hands resting on the chair-back balled into fists.

But then, exercising the same kind of control Joanna had used earlier, he expelled his breath. 'I didn't come here to talk about Sam,' he said tautly, meeting her gaze. 'My father's dying.'

Joanna gulped. She couldn't help it. Ryan Macallister had always appeared invincible to her. It scarcely seemed credible that he was mortal, like the rest of them.

Even so, he had never been any friend of hers, and her dark brows rose without sympathy. 'Is that supposed to mean something to me?'

Cole regarded her grimly. 'He wants to see you.'

'To see me?' Joanna's voice came out several degrees higher than normal, but Cole only nodded.

'That's what I said.'

Joanna caught her breath. 'You can't be serious.'

'Why not?'

'Why not?' She made a sound of disbelief. 'Why— he doesn't even *like* me!'

Cole's eyes dropped. 'Maybe he does,' he said, picking up the spoon that was lying beside the unused place-setting in front of him. 'Maybe he doesn't.' He spun the spoon between his fingers. 'In any case, he says he wants to see you, and that's all there is to it.'

'You wish!' Joanna stared at him incredulously. 'If you think I'm going to give up my holiday to go and see an old man who never even gave me the time of day, if he could help it, you're very much mistaken!'

Cole looked up, and the blue eyes were as cold as steel between narrowed lids. 'Are you really that hard?' he asked, his lips curling contemptuously. 'God, Ma said you wouldn't come, but I didn't believe her.'

'Believe it,' said Joanna flatly, pressing her hands down on the table and getting to her feet. 'I wish I could say it's been a pleasure, Cole, but lying was never my strong point!'

'Like hell!'

Cole had kicked the chair out from under him, and was up on his feet to confront her, before she could make good her escape. And, even though she stood a good five feet nine inches in her ankle boots, she was no match for his six feet plus. Add to that broad shoulders, a flat stomach, and long muscular legs, and she could see no means of retreat. Short of causing a scene, of course, and Joanna didn't want to do that, when this was only the second morning of her holiday.

'Isn't this rather ridiculous, Cole?' she asked, looking up at him rather tensely. 'What do you hope to achieve? You can't force me to go with you.'

'Can't I?'

Cole's response was predictable enough, but it lacked conviction, and Joanna realised that, for all his belligerence, he was unsure of his ground. It gave her a feeling of triumph just watching him—a rippling sensation of pleasure she hadn't felt before.

'I think you'd better get out of my way,' she said, not afraid to meet his gaze. 'What can you do to me—that you haven't already done?'

'Son of a——'

Cole bit off the expletive, but not before Joanna had glimpsed the raw frustration in his eyes. It was the first time she ever remembered him being at a loss for words, and there was a tantalising enjoyment in watching him squirm.

'So, if you'll excuse me——'

Brushing his chest with just the tips of her fingers, Joanna edged around him—and he let her. It was rather like baiting a tiger, she thought, the fluttering excitement in her throat threatening to choke her. It was so intoxicating that she felt quite high, and she could hardly contain herself as she deliberately sauntered across the terrace and into the hotel.

She knew his eyes followed her. She could feel them, boring into her back, as she swayed provocatively between the tables. And she was glad he would see nothing to betray the emotional trauma he had once wrought in her life. Her figure was as slim now as it had ever been, due as much to hard work as careful dieting. Her legs were long, and shown to some advantage in the frayed Bermudas she was wearing with a buttoned vest. Even her hair had the shiny patina of good health, longer now than she used to wear it, and caught at her nape in a silver barrette.

Of course, she came down to earth again as quickly as she had gone up. As soon as she was inside the glass screens, which had been folded back to allow free access between the indoor and outdoor sections of the restaurant, the sense of exhilaration she had felt while she was with Cole quickly abated. Besides, once the desire to thwart his plans had been accomplished, she was troubled by an annoying twinge of conscience. Whatever Cole thought, she was not as hard as he imagined. And, although it was true that Ryan Macallister had never accepted her as Cole's wife, he was an old man, and dying, if Cole was to be believed.

She paused in the lobby of the hotel, not sure now of what she wanted to do. She had been intending to get a book from her room and spend the morning sitting in the sun, but her confrontation with her ex-husband had left her disturbed and restless.

She needed her swimsuit anyway, so, forcing thoughts of Cole aside, she took the lift up to her room. She was on the fourth floor, just one below the penthouse suites. She had a large room, that was part-sitting-room, part-bedroom, with a wide balcony overlooking the Atlantic. All the rooms had balconies, but they were made private by the solid walls that divided them.

As she stripped off her vest and shorts and put on a scarlet *maillot*, Joanna couldn't help wondering where Cole was staying. She guessed he must have flown down from Charleston yesterday evening, and it was infinitely possible that he was staying at this hotel. But he had probably just booked in for one night. He had no doubt expected to persuade her to fly back with him later today.

She sighed, regarding her reflection in the long closet mirrors, without really noticing how well the strapless swimsuit looked. Perhaps she should just sunbathe on her balcony this morning, she was thinking. She didn't think Cole would know her actual room number, and even if he did he was unlikely to come looking for her.

Then she frowned. No, she told herself firmly. She was not going to run away from this. She had proved she could challenge Cole and get away with it. Why shouldn't she do so again, if it was necessary? It didn't matter what he said, or what he thought of her. She was a free woman. She could do what she liked.

In any case, she added, in a less than radical afterthought, Cole was unlikely to hang around, once he realised she meant what she said. It was early May, after all. A busy time of the year for him. And if his father was seriously ill——

But Joanna refused to think about it. She would not allow herself to feel guilty about a man who had always hated her, and her beliefs. Dear God, he had even destroyed his own son in his efforts to get what he wanted!

The phone rang as she was pulling an outsize T-shirt over her head. The baggy cotton garment barely skimmed her thighs, but its shoulders would keep her cool if the sun got too hot. It served the dual purpose of covering her swimsuit and providing protection, and she liked it better than some custom-made jacket.

When the phone rang, she hastily jammed her arms into the sleeves, and tugged it down around her. Then, halfway to answer the call, she halted. What if it was Cole? She was not sure she was ready yet for another altercation. She needed time to build her defences. She wasn't sure she was as immune to his censure as she thought.

But the realisation that it was more likely to be her mother, calling to make sure everything was OK, forced her to think again. Neither of her parents had been particularly keen on her taking this holiday alone, not to mention travelling so far from her home in London. In spite of her abortive marriage to Cole—or perhaps because of it—they had become increasingly protective, and, although she had phoned them on her arrival two days ago, they probably wanted an update on her movements.

Even so, there was a definite edge to her tone as she picked up the receiver, and the woman's voice that greeted her revealed a similar tension.

'Jo? Jo, darling, is that you? Oh, God, you sound so clear. Are you really thousands of miles away?'

Joanna's relief was almost palpable, and, running her tongue over her dry lips, she smoothed one damp palm down the seam of her T-shirt. But with the relief came a kindling of resentment towards her caller, and her voice was only slightly warmer as she answered, 'Yes. Yes, Grace, it's me. A sitting duck, as you expected.'

'Oh, Jo!' Grace sounded anxious now. 'I know what you must be thinking, but try to understand my position. Ryan is my brother-in-law, after all. When—when Cole asked where you were, I had to tell him.'

Joanna absorbed this in silence. Although she still resented the fact that Grace had betrayed her whereabouts, without even clearing it with her first, she wasn't unmindful of Grace's family responsibilities. Oh, it was easy enough to dismiss them by reminding herself that Grace's marriage to Ryan Macallister's brother had been no more successful than her own, but the truth was Grace was more dependent on the Macallisters than she was. Grace and Luke Macallister had two sons, Evan and Luke Junior. If she wanted to continue seeing her sons on a regular basis, she couldn't afford to offend the man who could deny her that privilege.

'Jo? Jo, are you still there?'

Grace's worried tones brought Joanna's attention back to the phone. It was her own fault really, she thought. As soon as her marriage to Cole broke up, she should have found herself another agent. But she had known Grace for almost ten years. Grace had recognised her talent long before the water-colours she produced became popular. Heavens, it was through Grace that she had met Cole—though the virtues of that particular introduction had long since been debased. Nevertheless, she was fond of Grace, she owed her a lot, and it wasn't fair to expect her to jeopardise her relationship with her own flesh and blood.

'Yes, I'm still here, Grace,' Joanna answered now, expelling her breath on a long sigh. 'OK, I forgive you. I suppose you didn't have a lot of choice. But, dammit, you should have warned me! I couldn't believe it when I saw Cole across the terrace.'

Grace made a sound of surprise. 'You've seen Cole?'

Joanna frowned. 'Of course.' She paused. 'What did you expect?'

'Oh—I don't know.' Grace sounded doubtful. 'When he phoned, I got the impression he didn't want to leave Tidewater at this particular time.'

Joanna shrugged. 'Well, he must have changed his mind.'

Grace hesitated. 'And are you going back with him?'

'No.'

'No?' Grace sounded dismayed. 'But Jo, Ryan's dying!'

'So?' Joanna refused to allow the other woman to influence her.

'He has cancer,' Grace persisted. 'According to Cole, the doctors give him a few weeks at most. Jo, he is Cole's father. Can't you find it in your heart to feel some compassion? I know you and he have had your differences, but——'

'Differences!' Joanna almost spat the word. 'Grace, that man and I did not have *differences*! We were totally opposed to one another in every way. Ryan Macallister doesn't deserve anyone's compassion. He's a twisted, evil man!'

Grace sighed. 'You really hate him, don't you?'

'Wouldn't you? *Don't* you?'

'Not hate, no.' Grace was tentative. 'Oh, I know what you're going to say. If Ryan hadn't made such a big thing of my wanting some independence, Luke would never have found the guts, strength—call it what you will—to make that ultimatum. But Jo, it was Luke who made me choose between staying at Tidewater, and vegetating, or making a life for myself. Ryan might have fashioned the bullets, my dear, but Luke fired them.'

'Yes, but——'

'Hear me out, Jo. I want you to know I haven't regretted what I did. Not really. Oh, I miss the boys, of course, but it's not as if they were babies when I left. And I've had a good life here. Running the gallery, becoming Ray's partner. He and I have more in common than Luke and I ever did. Luke was different. He was exciting. And I don't deny that Ray and I—well, we don't have the same kind of relationship. Ours is more—intellectual, if you know what I mean. But I'm not bitter. I have everything I need. I can afford to feel pity.'

'Well, I can't.'

Joanna pressed her lips together, and Grace breathed deeply. 'No,' she conceded, after a moment. 'No, I see that. I suppose I'd forgotten how much you love Cole——'

'*Loved*!' Joanna amended harshly. 'You'd forgotten how much I loved Cole. Not any more. That love died when they killed Nathan. Or did you forget about him, too?'

There was silence for a while, and when Grace spoke again there was regret in her voice. 'No,' she said softly. 'No, of course I haven't forgotten Nathan. I'm sorry, Jo. Naturally you must do what you think best.'

Conversely, Joanna felt guilty now. Oh, not about Ryan Macallister, she consoled herself, but perhaps she had been hard on Grace.

'It doesn't matter,' she said, forcing her mind on to other things. 'Um—how are the arrangements for the exhibition going? Do you think it's going to attract enough interest?'

'Are you kidding?' Grace responded eagerly, evidently as anxious as Joanna to turn their conversation on to a business footing. 'I've already had acceptances to the opening from all the most important critics, and even Howard Jennings has agreed to make an appearance.'

'Oh, good.'

Joanna tried to summon some enthusiasm for the news that the editor and presenter of a monthly television arts programme was apparently interested enough to attend, but somehow the importance of the exhibition had been blurred. In spite of all she had said, the image of Cole's father, sick and dying of that most pernicious of diseases, would not go away, and she was inordinately grateful when Grace said she would have to go, and rang off.

But, if she had hoped that by severing the connection with Grace she could sever all thoughts of the Macallisters, she was mistaken. Memories of Cole, and his father, and Tidewater just kept on coming back, and it was with an angry sense of resentment that she snatched up the bag containing her book, sun-screen, and dark glasses, and left the room.

CHAPTER TWO

THE sun was soothing. It was hard to think of anything with its rays beating against her closed eyelids, and bringing a film of perspiration to her supine body. It was hot beside the pool, hotter than on the beach, where there was at least a breeze off the water to temper the humidity. But Joanna welcomed the numbing effects of the heat, and the mindless lethargy it engendered.

Her hands uncurled against the cream towel she had spread over the slatted sun-bed, and she arched one leg in an unknowingly provocative pose. Oh, yes, she decided contentedly, this was definitely the life! She refused to think about anything, except what she was going to have for lunch.

She had chosen a chair in a secluded corner of the pool deck. It wasn't that she was unsociable. It was just that she had no wish to appear in need of company. She knew perfectly well that a woman alone often attracted unwelcome attention from the opposite sex, and indulging in any kind of holiday flirtation was not what she had come here for. At home, she did accept an occasional invitation to dinner, or the theatre, but that was different. On the whole, her escorts knew that she was not interested in any serious commitment, and if any of them showed they would prefer a more intimate relationship they were quickly discarded. She liked men, but at a distance. She was polite, and friendly, but nothing more. She had been hurt badly once, and she had no intention of repeating the experience.

Consequently, she was not a little irritated when someone came to occupy the chair next to hers. Through half-closed lids, she glimpsed the cuffs of dark blue swimming-shorts, and brown, muscular legs that curved beneath the cuffs into tight masculine buttocks.

Damn, she thought, closing her eyes again, and pretending she was unaware of him. There were at least fifty other sun-beds set at different angles around the pool. And surely among them were other single women, who would be flattered to receive his attention. Why couldn't he have chosen one of them? She wanted to relax, not spend her time fending off passes.

The seductive stroke of a cool finger along her arm brought her eyes open with a start. The light, sensitive touch was unwillingly sensual, but she was too angry to admit its effect. What cheek! she thought furiously, pushing herself up. Was it too much to expect that she should be left alone?

Jerking down her sunglasses, which she had been wearing as a kind of surrogate head-band, she turned her incensed gaze on the man beside her. And then her jaw sagged disbelievingly. It wasn't some pool-side Romeo who was resting on the chair beside hers. It was Cole!

'Hi,' he said non-committally. 'I'm pleased to see you don't encourage boarders.'

Joanna's anger floundered. 'What are you doing here, Cole?' she exclaimed. 'I thought you'd be on the next flight back to South Carolina.'

'Hmm. I guess you did.' Cole stretched his long legs comfortably, and laced his hands beneath his head. 'Well, as you can see, I'm still here.'

'I won't change my mind, you know.'

Joanna's response was half peevish, and she wished she hadn't felt the need to defend herself, when Cole merely shifted to a more restful position.

'I haven't asked you to, have I?' he countered, looking up at her through the sun-bleached tips of his lashes. 'Relax, Jo. It's much too hot to fuel all that adrenalin.'

Joanna pressed her lips together mutinously, trying to regain her composure. Now that she was assured that no one was trying to proposition her, she ought to be able to rekindle her sense of well-being.

But, of course, she couldn't. Although she determinedly lay down again, the feeling of tranquillity had left her. She felt on edge, and agitated, and far too aware of the man on the sun-bed beside her.

His arm was only inches from hers, she observed covertly, tautly muscled, and displaying the tiny tattoo of a venomous bushmaster, which he had had etched when he was just a boy, and for which, he had told her, his father had soundly beaten him. The muscle flexed, as she watched it, tightening and hardening, before relaxing once again. The skin that covered the rest of his arm was brown and smooth and flawless, almost hairless, and lightly sheened with sweat.

Without any volition on her part, her body responded to the sensual appeal of his. The sight of his bare chest, with its flat nipples, and light dusting of hair, disturbed her. She found her eyes following the provocative arrowing of hair that disappeared beneath the elasticated waistband of his shorts. His restless movements had inched the waistband of the shorts down below his navel, and his pelvis made a cradle of his sex.

God! She tore her eyes away, and stared blindly across the pool. What was the matter with her? she chided, as her hands coiled into tight fists. It wasn't as if Cole's naked body was any novelty to her. She had lived with him for more than two years, for heaven's sake! She had seen him in every pose and attitude, in every state of undress. He had a beautiful lean body— a perfect specimen of American manhood. It was a pity the contents didn't live up to the wrapping!

'Do you want a drink?'

She was so tied up with her thoughts that Cole's first question didn't register. 'I—beg your pardon?'

'I said—do you want a drink?' he repeated, propping himself up on his elbow, drawing up one leg, and half turning towards her. 'There's a waitress making a tour of the deck, taking orders. I thought you might like something long and cold and refreshing.'

'Oh——' Joanna swallowed, and explored her dry lips with her tongue. 'Well, yes. I think I will have some lemonade. But I'll get my own. You don't have to bother.'

'It's no bother,' Cole assured her, swinging his feet to the ground. He moved swiftly, so that by the time the bikini-clad waitress reached them he was standing up, and Joanna saw to her chagrin that his southern courtesy did not go unnoticed.

'You didn't have to stand up,' she muttered irritably, as he resumed his seat, and Cole's mouth tilted.

'No, I know,' he agreed, brushing an insect from his thigh with a lazy hand. 'But it costs nothing to be polite.'

'Would you have stood up if it had been a man?' she persisted, and Cole's lips parted to reveal a row of even white teeth.

'I guess,' he said, his eyes leaving hers to move insolently over her body. 'What's the matter, Jo? Something eating you?'

Joanna shifted uneasily beneath his taunting gaze, and she was aware that she was still aroused from her thoughts earlier. Her own nipples were as taut as buttons, and she tugged surreptitiously at the front of her swimsuit to hide their provocative display.

Unable to think of an answer sharp enough to puncture his mocking self-confidence, she turned her head, and pretended to watch the antics of two young people in the pool. They were teenagers, she guessed, holidaying together for the first time, and from the way the girl draped herself around her companion they were not ignorant of each other's bodies. There was an intimacy between them that spoke of long nights exploring the intricacies of love. She and Cole had once explored those same intricacies, she remembered. During those long southern nights, before things started to go wrong . . .

The waitress returned with two tall glasses of lemonade, liberally spiked with ice. Cole took one for himself, and held the other out towards Joanna, and although she was loath to take anything from him it would have been childish to refuse. So, sitting up, cross-legged, she took the perspex tumbler from him, drinking from it thirstily, before tipping her head back on her shoulders, and luxuriating in the intense heat.

Cole was still sitting sideways on the sun-bed, legs spread, bare feet resting on the tiled surface of the pool-deck. It meant she was constantly aware of his eyes upon her but, despite her irritation, she supposed his presence was deterring any unwelcome attention.

'You look good,' he said suddenly, and her eyes jerked towards his before she could prevent them.

'Thank you,' she returned, striving for a careless tone as she took herself in hand again. 'So do you. Sammy-Jean's evidently doing something right.'

Cole's expression hardened for a moment, but then he returned to the attack. 'You always were a beautiful woman,' he murmured. 'And, if anything, you look better now than you did when we got married.'

'Then I must be doing something right, too,' declared Joanna shortly, impatient at the wave of colour that swept into her neck at his words. 'Living in London isn't all bad, whatever you think. Our climate may not be as good as yours, but it has its compensations.'

Cole's brows arched for a moment, and then he looked down at his drink, resting in hands hanging loosely between his thighs. 'I guess it does,' he conceded at last. 'I'm sure Grace would agree with you.'

'I'm sure she would.' Joanna nodded. But she didn't like this conversation. It wasn't what Cole was saying that troubled her exactly. But the tone he was using did. He was so polite. His lazy southern drawl scraped across her nerves, like a nail over raw silk, and every time he looked at her she grew more and more tense.

'Um—how—how's your mother?' she asked, hoping to divert the conversation away from herself, and Cole lifted his head.

'Ma's OK.' His eyes skimmed her mouth, and although she had just drunk about a quarter of a pint of lemonade Joanna's lips felt parched. 'She's getting older, like the rest of us. But she still works just as hard as ever.'

'And—and Ben and Joe?' Joanna felt compelled to keep him talking about his family. 'And the twins? I bet Charley can swim now, can't she? Did they start high school yet? Oh, yes, of course, they must have done.'

Cole regarded her between narrowed lids. 'Are you really that interested?' he queried, his brooding gaze bringing a deepening of colour in her cheeks. 'Sure, Ben and Joe are fine. Joe's married now, and his wife's expecting their first baby. Charley and Donna started high school last year, and Sandy's going to join them come fall.' He paused. 'I guess that about covers it, wouldn't you say?'

Joanna bent her head, the weight of her hair sliding over one shoulder to expose the vulnerable curve of her neck. 'I was just being—polite, that's all,' she said, half defensively. 'I—like your brothers and sisters. And, I used to think that they liked me.'

'They did.' Cole shook the ice around in his empty tumbler. 'Charley often used to talk about the time you and she got stuck out on Palmer's Island. If you hadn't swum back to get help, you might both have been swept away.'

'Oh——' Joanna made a deprecating gesture. 'You'd already discovered we were missing. When the boat was washed on to the bank, you'd have guessed where we were.'

'Maybe not soon enough,' he insisted, and Joanna felt a remembered sense of apprehension. She could still recall how scared she had been in the water, fighting her way against the current, feeling her arms getting weaker by the minute. She had been unable to

stand, when she hauled herself out of the river. If Cole
and his brothers hadn't been searching for them, it
might still have been too late. The flooding torrent of
the Tidewater River had left Palmer's Island under
several feet of water for hours. No one could have sur-
vived its fury, least of all ten-year-old Charley, who
couldn't even swim.

Joanna grimaced now, unwilling to think of that
near-tragedy, and Cole stretched out his hand towards
her. She thought for one heart-stopping moment that
he was going to touch her, and she instinctively drew
back against the chair. But, although his lips flattened
for a moment, revealing his awareness of her reaction,
all he did was lift the empty tumbler out of her hand.

'I'll get rid of these,' he said, dropping one inside the
other, and while she tried to recover her self-possession
he sauntered across the deck to dump the tumblers.

By the time she heard the depression of his chair's
plastic slats, she was once again reclining on her towel,
on her stomach this time, with her eyes closed, and her
face turned deliberately away from him. Surely he
would get the message, she thought tensely. She didn't
want to have to spell it out for him again. He was
wasting his time if he thought he could get her to
change her mind. They had a saying in the south, about
catching more bees with honey than with vinegar, but
if that was Cole's intention it wasn't going to work. He
was an attractive man, sure, and, even though she had
more reason than most to regret the fact, she wouldn't
have been a woman if she hadn't found him easy to
look at. But that was all. She wasn't attracted to him.
Not any more.

'You're going to get burned,' his lazy voice observed, revealing his skin was thicker than even she had thought, and Joanna clamped her jaws together.

'No, I'm not,' she retorted, through her teeth. 'My skin's too dark, remember?'

'It's also used to a colder climate,' Cole replied, and she heard him get up from his chair again.

God! Joanna lay completely still for a moment, and then, unable to withstand the suspense a moment longer, she rolled over on to her back—just as Cole was lowering his weight on to the side of her slatted mattress. It was just by a swift removal of her arm that she avoided being sat on, and her eyes sparkled indignantly at his uninvited presumption.

'What the hell do you——?' she was beginning, when Cole showed her the tube of sun-screening cream in his hand.

'This is yours, isn't it?' he asked, and she guessed he had rifled it from her bag. 'Turn over,' he added, unscrewing the cap and squeezing a curl of its contents into his palm. 'There's no point in torturing yourself just to spite me.'

Joanna pressed her lips together and stared up at him, resentment oozing from every pore. The last thing she wanted was his help, in anything. And she certainly didn't want him touching her. But once again he had her at a disadvantage, caught between the desire to show her real feelings, and the knowledge that by doing so she would be handing him all the cards.

So, instead of snatching the cream out of his hand and hurling it into the pool, she forced a tight smile and obediently rolled over again. Let him do his worst, she thought, stifling her angry reaction against the towel. After all, although her skin didn't tan, it did burn sometimes, and she could do without that aggravation as well.

Cole's hands were amazingly cool against her hot flesh. Of course, he had just been handling the tumblers containing the ice, she reminded herself grimly, as his long fingers slid across her shoulders, and his thumbs found the nubby column of her spine. She found it was important to keep a sense of proportion, as his probing hands found every inch of exposed skin. She was relieved she wasn't wearing a bikini. At least the modest *maillot* left her some dignity.

But not a lot, she had to concede, as the sinuous brush of his fingers began to lull her into a false sense of security. It would be so easy, she thought, to go with the flow; to allow her flesh to respond to the sensuous touch of his; to admit she was enjoying his expert ministrations. Because of the limitations of the sunbed, his leg was wedged beside her hip, and although the swimsuit protected the upper half of her pelvis his hair-roughened thigh was against the exposed curve of her bottom. It meant that every stroke of his hands on her shoulders brought a corresponding increase of pressure against her hip, and the images that evoked were all sexual . . .

'I—think that will do,' she declared firmly, arching her back away from his fingers, and getting up on to her knees. 'I'm not planning to stay out here that much longer.'

'No?' With a resigned shrug of his shoulders, Cole moved obediently back to his own chair. 'What are you planning to do, then?'

Joanna didn't look at him. 'I think that's my business, don't you?'

'I guess.' Cole screwed the top back on the tube of sun-cream and dropped it carelessly into her bag. 'Only askin', lady.'

'And I'm telling you, it's none of your business,' said Joanna shortly. 'In any case, don't you have a plane to catch, or something?'

'Not until tomorrow,' Cole replied, wiping his greasy hands over his knees. 'Sorry.'

'I should have guessed.' Joanna's impatient gaze darted over him. 'You obviously came prepared.'

'You mean these?' Cole hooked a thumb into the waistband of his shorts. 'I bought them this morning in the shop, here in the hotel. Along with a couple of pairs of underpants, and a fresh shirt.'

Joanna's lips pursed. 'Really.'

'Yes, really.' Cole inclined his head. 'It wasn't my intention to stay away from Tidewater any longer than I had to.'

Joanna dropped her sunglasses down on to her nose again. She had pushed them up into her hair, while she had been lying on her stomach. But now she felt the need for them again, and the doubtful protection they provided.

'I guess this is a good place to paint, huh?' Cole murmured, gazing narrow-eyed towards the ocean. 'Grace told me you've got an exhibition coming up.'

'Oh—yes.' Joanna wondered what else Grace had told him. 'The—er—the opening's a couple of weeks after I get back.'

'A couple of weeks?' His eyes flickered. 'Maybe I should buy a ticket. Get myself an investment for the future.'

'You're not serious!'

Joanna's reaction was unguarded, and he turned to look at her with mild enquiry. 'Why not?' he countered. 'I can tell everyone it was painted by my ex-wife. Should add a lick of glamour to the price, if I ever want to sell it.'

'That's sick!'

'Is it? Why? Just 'cause maybe I wan' somethin' to 'member you by?'

'Don't talk like that!'

Cole's brows arched. 'Like what?'

'Like you didn't know better,' retorted Joanna crossly. 'Oh—do what you like. I can't stop you.'

His shoulders hunched, and when he spoke again his voice was low and husky. 'You could have dinner with me tonight.'

'Have dinner with you?' Joanna was taken aback.

'Sure. Why not?'

'Well——' Joanna floundered. 'I—can't.'

'You having dinner with someone else?'

'No.'

The response was automatic. But she could hardly say she was, when if he walked into the restaurant he would find her eating alone. Too late she realised she could have gone out to eat, or ordered room service, but she had answered without thinking. In any case, she didn't see why she had to make an excuse. It wasn't as if she wanted to have dinner with him.

'You afraid to eat with me?' he suggested slyly, and her resentment flared anew.

'No,' she denied tautly. 'Why would I be? But I don't think your father, or Sammy-Jean, would approve of our socialising, do you?'

'And that's why you're refusing? Because you don't want to offend my father?'

'No!' Joanna tore the dark glasses off her nose, and stared at him frustratedly. 'Cole, why are you doing this? You know you don't really want to have dinner with me at all.'

'Don't I?' His deep blue eyes ranged disturbingly over her flushed face. 'Maybe I do. For old times' sake. What do you say?'

Joanna's hands clenched around the stems of her glasses. Of course, she did know why he was doing this, she told herself. Cole was nothing if not tenacious, and he had evidently got it into his head that sooner or later she would crack. The small talk, the lemonade, and the massage were all intended to soften her up, to make her more receptive, when he mentioned his father's illness again. He had even bitten the bullet and asked about the exhibition. That must have really galled him. Her work had always been a source of conflict in the past.

Her lips twisted. So how far was he prepared to go, to gain his own ends? If she agreed to have dinner with him, what then? He could hardly talk about something as serious as cancer over the red snapper. So, when did he intend to make his next move? And how?

An imp of vengeance stirred inside her. It might be amusing to find out. In spite of the casual way he had handled the conversation this morning, she hadn't forgotten his reaction when she turned the tables on him. So long as she was on the defensive, he had nothing to fear. But if she decided to play a different game...

Could she do it? That was what she had to ask herself. She hadn't to forget that people who played with fire sometimes got burned. But she was over Cole, completely and irrevocably. Her body might still respond to the sexuality of his, but her mind was not involved. And how she chose to behave was no one's business but her own.

Taking a deep breath, she came to a decision. 'All right,' she said, sliding the dark glasses back into place. 'For old times' sake. Why not?'

Protected by the glasses, she caught the fleeting trace of surprise that crossed his face at her words. Evidently, he had expected it to be harder to get her to change her mind. None the less, he recovered himself with admirable efficiency, and his lazy smile tugged the corners of his mouth upwards.

'OK,' he said, making no objection when she began to gather her belongings together with the obvious intention of leaving. 'I'll meet you in the lobby of the hotel at seven o'clock, right?'

'Right.'

Joanna forced a matching smile. But her expression was distinctly cat-like, as she negligently made her departure.

CHAPTER THREE

JOANNA decided to skip lunch, and go into town. She had intended to get a snack from the poolside bar, but the prospect that she might run into Cole again before the evening decided her against it.

Besides, she hadn't been into Nassau since her arrival. The international airport on New Providence was situated at the north-western end of the island, and the Coral Beach Hotel was on the coast that lay between the airport and the town of Nassau. The previous day she had spent recovering from her jet lag, and basking in her new-found freedom. But today she felt too strung-up by the thought of the evening ahead to relax anywhere. She needed action, and distraction, and the chance to spend some of the dollars she had brought with her.

After taking a shower to remove the combined effects of the heat and the protective cream Cole had applied, Joanna dressed in the shorts and soft boots she had worn earlier. But instead of the vest she donned a loose-fitting T-shirt. No point in risking sunburn, she told herself sardonically. Not when she wanted to look her best that evening.

She took a taxi from the hotel into town. The garrulous Bahamian driver dropped her in Bay Street, and she spent a pleasant couple of hours browsing through the shops and the Straw Market. She bought herself a length of vividly patterned cotton, to wear sarong-wise around the pool, and a chunky handful of bracelets, sculpted from shells, that clattered attractively every time she moved her wrist. She also treated herself to a new swimsuit, a bikini this time, patterned with the many exotic flowers of the islands.

Before going back to the hotel, she bought herself a can of Coke, and strolled down to the harbour to drink it. A huge cruise liner was tied up at Prince George's Wharf, and she sat for a while on the sea-wall, watching the activity around the ship.

Passengers came and went, stores were taken on board, members of the crew took time out to stretch their legs on dry land, and local youths on bicycles milled about the quay. If she had had her sketch pad with her, Joanna knew, she would not have been able to resist trying to capture the scene on paper. There was so much colour and excitement, and when she eventually left the harbour the images were still buzzing inside her head.

Perhaps she ought to buy herself a sketch pad, she thought, strolling up into Rawson Square. She had no doubt she would be able to get what she wanted along Bay Street. Although it wasn't pretentious, it was one of the most comprehensive shopping streets in the world.

But then she shook her head and hailed a taxi to take her back to the hotel. This was supposed to be a holiday, she chided herself. Just because Cole had come, upsetting her carefully arranged schedule, and reminding her that she had once used her work as a means of escape, was no reason to go rushing for the charcoal. She could handle Cole now. She had proved it earlier. And this evening he would realise she was no longer the vulnerable girl he had married and divorced.

Selecting what to wear that evening was rather more difficult than she had expected. While she wanted to look provocative, she did not want to appear tacky. Sexy clothes were all very well, but it was all too easy to go over the top. Luckily, she had gone shopping before she left England, so her choice was not limited. But whether it should be a mini cocktail dress, or a slinky trouser suit, was not an easy decision to make.

She eventually chose to wear a dress. A silk-satin sheath in shades of green and purple that complimented her dark colouring, and brought out the tawny highlights in her eyes. It was short, barely reaching mid-thigh, and the on-the-shoulder, off-the-shoulder neckline exposed the creamy beauty of her skin. She wore no bra or tights, only a lacy brief, for modesty's sake. It made her look—interesting, she decided. Thank God the extra inches she had acquired after the divorce, when eating and drinking had seemed her only consolations, had all been coaxed away by careful dieting. These days, the energy she gave to her work burned off any unwanted calories. And attending a weekly work-out class kept her body lean and supple.

She left her dark hair loose, securing it away from her face on one side with combs. Although it was silky straight, it was thick and shining, and swung smoothly against her shoulders. Like the rest of her, it was sleek and healthy, and she spared a moment's unwilling consideration for the man who'd sent Cole here.

If the thought of how what she was planning to do might affect Sammy-Jean disturbed her, she dismissed it. Sammy-Jean had shown no qualms about seducing her husband, so wouldn't it be ironic now if she could return the compliment? Not that she wanted Cole back again, she assured herself. But taking him away from Sammy-Jean did have a certain malicious appeal.

She needed very little make-up. Her lashes were naturally dark, and only a little dusky eyeshadow was needed to add mystery to the depths of her eyes. A trace of blusher over her cheekbones gave a little colour to her face, and a shiny amber lip-salve enhanced the sensitive fullness of her mouth.

When she viewed her reflection in the mirror, before going downstairs, she was reasonably content with her appearance. She looked young, and sexy, but tantalisingly remote.

The lobby of the Coral Beach Hotel was an atrium, arching to a high, glass-vaulted ceiling. The several floors of rooms curved round the central area, which served as both reception and shopping mall. Tall plants and flowering shrubs filled every available space, with a stone-carved fountain providing a focal point.

As Joanna came down the staircase from the mezzanine, she could see Cole waiting by the fountain. She had chosen to get out of the lift at the floor above ground level, so that she might observe him before he saw her. It was a careful ploy, born of her desire to control every aspect of the evening they were to spend together. Besides, it gave her the opportunity to compose her entrance. Streaming out of the lift, with a throng of other passengers, right where he was standing, was not what she had in mind.

As she had hoped, he saw her before she reached the bottom of the stairs. His searching gaze alighted on her slender figure, as she negotiated the last three steps, and although she affected not to have seen him she was instantly aware of his sharp reaction. He didn't come to meet her, but his eyes followed every move she made. Much the way the snake he had tattooed on his shoulder watched its victim, she mused fancifully. But that was not a comparison she wanted to make.

He was wearing a jacket, she noticed, a concession to the fact that it was evening. He certainly didn't need it, even in the air-conditioned lobby of the hotel. Bahamian nights were deliciously warm and inviting. But the more exclusive restaurants insisted on this small formality, so evidently they were dining somewhere expensive.

And God, didn't he look good! she acknowledged objectively. So good, in fact, that for a moment she doubted her ability to pull this off. But then the reluctant admiration she saw in his eyes restored her confidence. Even if he had deserted her bed for Sammy-Jean's, he was not indifferent to her. Though she guessed he would hate to admit it.

'Hi,' she said, as she closed the space between them. 'I hope I haven't kept you waiting.'

Cole shrugged, his broad shoulders moving sinuously beneath the beige twill of his jacket. 'I had nothing better to do,' he said, his eyes flickering swiftly over the tantalising curve of her breasts, exposed by the dipping neckline of the dress. Then, looking beyond her, he added, 'I didn't realise there were guest rooms on the mezzanine.'

Joanna's dark brows arched enquiringly. 'Does it matter?'

'You walked down from the mezzanine,' Cole reminded her sardonically. 'Funny. I got the impression you were staying on one of the higher floors.'

Joanna hid a smile. Evidently, Cole had made it his business to find out exactly where she was staying, but she had been prepared for his question, and her lips tilted charmingly.

'I made a mistake,' she lied ruefully. 'The lift stopped and I got out.' She grimaced. 'Silly me!'

'Hmm.'

Cole's grunt of assent was hardly sympathetic, but Joanna had achieved what she wanted to achieve, and she could afford to be generous. 'Does it matter?' she exclaimed, looking up at him disarmingly. 'I'm here now. So—where are we eating?'

Cole's mouth flattened. 'I thought we might eat at the Commodore Club. They have an excellent restaurant, and you might like to visit the casino later.'

Joanna nodded. 'Sounds good to me.' She tucked her leather bag against her side, and slid her fingers round his arm. 'Shall we go?'

The muscles of his upper arm were taut beneath her grip. She sensed he would like to release himself, and she wondered how he had expected her to behave. It was obvious he was confused by her apparent willingness to co-operate, and he was wary of her appearance, and the provocation it presented.

A row of taxis waited on the forecourt of the hotel, and a black-suited major-domo summoned one at Cole's request. Joanna climbed into the back of the cab unaided, smoothing down her tight skirt as she scrambled across the seat. She had noticed before that no one bothered to walk round the cabs, and get in at the opposite side. And Cole was no exception as he followed her inside.

But she noticed he kept his distance during the fifteen-minute ride to the Commodore Club. His dark-clad thigh—had he bought a whole wardrobe at the hotel shop?—rested on the worn leather upholstery, several inches away from hers. And, because the majority of taxis Joanna had seen were old American limousines, there was plenty of room.

Getting out of the taxi, he was obliged to offer her his hand. Whatever else he might be, Cole considered himself a gentleman. One of the South Carolina 'good ole boys', thought Joanna cynically. Just like his father, and his father before him.

Even so, putting her hand into Cole's was a disturbing experience. His hand was cool and firm, with calluses at the base of his fingers. And when those fingers curled around hers she was hard-pressed not to hold on.

But, even if she'd wanted to, Cole had to pay the fare. After helping her out, under the striped canopy of the club, he bent to speak to their driver. Then, returning his wallet to his hip pocket, he straightened, urging her into the foyer, with his hand in the small of her back.

It saved touching her skin, Joanna thought ruefully, as they stepped on to the escalator which would take them up to the bar and restaurant. She wondered what he was thinking. Somehow, she sensed she was not going to have it all her own way.

'Do you want a drink before we eat?' Cole asked, as they crossed the carpeted upper floor, and Joanna tilted her head.

'Mmm,' she said. 'Something long and cool, with a bite to it. What would you recommend?'

Cole's eyes glinted. 'I'm sure I'll think of something,' he said, guiding her towards an empty table. 'I seem to remember you had quite a fancy for mint-juleps. You used to down quite a few of them, while Pa and I were out in the fields.'

Joanna's lips tightened for a moment, as the memories his words evoked came back to haunt her. But when she looked at him none of her anguish showed in her face. You shouldn't have said that, Cole, she thought malevolently. I'm going to make you pay for every little dig you make!

'So I did,' she warbled now, and no one listening to her would have imagined the offence she had felt at his words. Bastard, she said silently, while her eyes sparkled with mirth. 'I was a pain, wasn't I? No wonder you preferred Sammy-Jean to me.'

It was Cole's turn to look bitter now, but the arrival of the waiter to take their order prevented him from venting his spleen. Besides, she guessed he couldn't be entirely sure exactly how she had meant it, and although he might suspect her motives he really had no proof.

'Bourbon and branch,' he said sourly, 'and something *sweet* for the lady. What do you suggest?'

'How about pineapple rum?' asked the waiter cheerfully. 'Pineapple rum, coconut rum, and pineapple juice, shaken over ice. Delicious!'

'It sounds it,' put in Joanna smoothly, crossing her legs, and running spread fingers over her knee. She smiled at the man. 'Cold, but hot. Exactly what I need.'

The waiter's eyes danced. 'Yes, sir,' he said, swinging on his heel, and walking back to the bar. 'A Valentine's Special, man,' he ordered from the barkeep. 'And make it real cold!'

Cole's eyes were far from friendly when he looked at Joanna again. 'Just what the hell do you think you're doing?' he demanded, his tone hard and explosive. 'Do you want everyone to think you're using?'

'Using?' Joanna's eyes widened innocently. 'Using what?'

'You know!' retorted Cole savagely. 'Hell, maybe you are. What would I know about it?'

Joanna's humour evaporated. 'I don't use—or shoot up—or mainline—or any of the other ways people take drugs,' she declared scornfully. 'I was having fun, that's all. *Fun*! Or have you forgotten the meaning of the word?'

Cole's mouth compressed. 'You weren't just having fun,' he argued. 'God, you were coming on to the man!'

Joanna's brief spurt of anger died. 'What's the matter, Cole?' she asked mockingly. 'You jealous?'

Their drinks came before Cole could make any response, but his brooding expression was eloquent of his feelings. Oh, this *was* fun, thought Joanna, a little breathlessly. Why had she never realised it was far more exciting to be bad?

The pineapple rum was delicious. It came complete with an assortment of tropical fruits, with a long curling straw to enable her to avoid the tiny striped umbrella. The umbrella bore the logo of the Commodore Club, and she was tempted to keep it as a souvenir of the evening.

'Have you and Sammy-Jean had any family yet?' she queried after a moment, risking Cole's displeasure yet again. She knew perfectly well that had Cole become a father she would have heard about it. Grace would surely have told her. But why should she avoid a subject that was clearly so exploitable?

Cole regarded her over the rim of his glass. 'No,' he said, and she could tell by his tone that he was not unaware of her intentions. 'But it's not for want of trying, if that's what you're implying.'

Joanna looked down into her drink. Her hands had tightened around the stem, and, noticing her white knuckles, she forced herself to relax. If she wasn't careful, the glass would break, and Cole would imagine he had scored a victory. What did it matter to her how many times Cole made love with Sammy-Jean? Sammy-Jean was his wife now, and she, Joanna, didn't give a damn!

'Something wrong?' Cole's blue eyes were smugly intent, and Joanna expelled her breath on a rueful sigh.

'No,' she said, deliberately wistful. 'I was just remembering how good you were in bed.'

'Good God!' Cole's jaw hardened. 'You don't give up, do you?' He swallowed the remainder of his drink in one violent gulp, and gestured for the waiter to bring him another. 'What do you want from me, Jo? *Blood*?'

Joanna knew a fleeting sense of conscience, but then the waiter arrived to replace Cole's glass, and she consoled herself by taking another mouthful of her own drink. But her lips around the pink straw were unconsciously provocative, and Cole uttered an imprecation as he lifted his bourbon to his mouth.

'You folks dinin'?' enquired the waiter, and at Cole's curt nod he flourished two enormous menus from under his arm. 'Take your time,' he added, his knowing gaze taking in the situation at a glance. 'I'll be back later to take your order.'

Propping her menu on the table in front of her, Joanna continued to enjoy her drink as she studied its contents. There was a vast array of dishes to choose from, with imported American steaks and locally caught seafood providing the main selections. There was fried chicken, too, prepared with the familiar 'peas 'n' rice', which was a national passion.

'What do you want?' asked Cole, after a few minutes, his tone cool and unfriendly, and Joanna felt a trace of regret.

'The grouper, I think,' she answered, mentioning the name of the most popular fish in the area. 'And melon, to begin with. I'm not very hungry.'

Cole acknowledged her choice with a brief inclination of his head, and the waiter, who had evidently been keeping an interested eye on their table, came to take their order.

Cole ordered the grouper, too, but with a salad starter. 'And bring the lady another of those,' he said, as Joanna set down her empty glass. 'And I'll have another bourbon.'

Joanna arched her brows, half in protest, but the waiter was already sauntering away between the tables. Besides, the drink had been delicious, she conceded. And fairly innocuous, too, judging by the clearness of her head.

There was silence between them for a while. Joanna could have broken it with some other audacious comment, but she realised she was in danger of alienating Cole completely, and that hadn't been her intention at all.

So, instead of sniping at him, she pretended an interest in their fellow guests, thanking the waiter for her drink when it came, without any further attempt to provoke her companion.

And, as she had half expected, Cole was eventually forced to say something. She guessed he was not unaware that their lack of communication had been noticed by the people at the next table, and as he had been the one to cause their isolation he chose to be the one to end it.

'Do you see much of Grace?' he asked, in a voice that would have cracked ice, and Joanna turned her gaze from a bowl of exotic plants to look at him.

'That depends,' she said, moistening her lips with the tip of her tongue.

'On what?'

The question was wrung from him, and Joanna smiled. 'On whether I'm working or not,' she declared smoothly. 'Grace is my agent. She's only interested in when I'm going to finish my next painting.'

'I'm sure that's not true.' Cole's tone had lost some of its chilliness. 'Grace always liked you. She considers you a friend.'

'Mmm.' Joanna stirred her drink with the straw. 'Well, let's say things have been a little strained between Grace and me, since we—broke up.'

Cole frowned. 'I don't believe it. Hell, I'd have thought you and she had a deal in common.'

'Would you?' Joanna looked at him through her lashes. 'You should know Grace won't have a word said against your father.'

Cole's mouth thinned. 'Unlike you, huh?'

'I don't have two sons whose livelihood is dependent on someone else's goodwill,' she countered lightly. 'Your father can't hurt me, Cole, and that must be a real source of aggravation to him.'

'I doubt if he cares that much, one way or the other,' retorted Cole bitterly. 'But you always had to face him down, didn't you? You'd never admit that sometimes he just might be right!'

'Like when he accused Nathan of sleeping with your wife?' she enquired tautly, and then, seeing the dark, tormented, expression her words had provoked, she quickly regressed. 'Forget I said that. It doesn't matter. He did us both a favour, didn't he? Oh—here's the waiter. Our table must be ready.'

CHAPTER FOUR

A FOUR-PIECE West Indian band was playing in the grill room, and Joanna was glad that the music negated any real obligation to talk while they were eating. Not that she ate a lot. The melon slid down smoothly enough, but the fish, which was served with a bouquet of vegetables, was rather more difficult to swallow. Instead, she turned to the wine Cole had ordered to accompany the meal, drinking several glasses of the chilled Californian Riesling.

There was a small dance-floor beyond the tables, where those guests who had finished their meal indulged in a little after-dinner exertion. Joanna spent most of her time watching them, uncaring for once if Cole was looking at her. With her elbow propped on the edge of the table and her chin cupped in one slender hand, she was unaware of the dreamy expression that crossed her face as she watched the swaying couples. For a while, she was completely oblivious of her surroundings, and it took a definite effort to concentrate again when the waiter came to ask if they wanted a dessert.

'Just coffee,' said Cole, without consulting her, and Joanna pulled an indignant face.

'I might have liked a dessert,' she pouted, and although she suspected he was only acting Cole's face softened.

'Coffee first, like back home,' he insisted wryly. 'I don't want to have to carry you out of here.'

'Would you do that?' she asked huskily, a feeling of heat sweeping over her, and although it wasn't all that easy to focus on his lean face she thought his eyes darkened at her words.

'If I have to,' he answered. 'Why? How do you feel?'

'Muzzy,' she admitted, emitting a rueful little laugh. 'Maybe I do need that coffee, after all.'

'You always were a cheap drunk,' he said, but for once there was no malice in his tone, and Joanna knew an overwhelming urge to make him as aware of her as she was of him.

Concentrating hard, she stretched out her hand and ran her fingers over his thigh. He jerked back automatically, but not before she had felt the instinctive tautening of muscle under her touch. From his groin to his knee, his leg stiffened defensively, and his lazy humour disappeared beneath a scowl of irritation.

But when he would have pushed her hand away, she thwarted him with an appealing smile. 'Dance with me,' she invited, turning her hand into his, and letting her thumb drift against his palm. 'Please, Cole. To show you're not mad at me. For old times' sake, as you said.'

He wanted to refuse. The evidence of that was clear in his face. And he resented her for using his words against him. But something—the memory of why he had come here, perhaps, or a desire to prove he was in control of his own destiny, who knew?—made him hesitate long enough for her to draw him to his feet.

'I don't dance,' he said, then, his voice clipped and harsh, 'I think we should get out of here. You need some fresh air.'

'Do I?'

Joanna swayed, most convincingly, which wasn't too surprising considering the wine had made her feel decidedly unsteady on her feet. But she could handle it, she told herself, not prepared to lose the advantage now.

'Yes, you do,' he muttered, as she continued to cling to his fingers. 'Jo, what do you think you're doing? This isn't the way to the exit.'

'I'll leave after we've danced,' declared Joanna firmly, tugging him after her. 'We used to dance before. Don't you remember?'

'That wasn't dancing,' snapped Cole, but Joanna's behaviour was attracting attention, and she could see he didn't like it.

'Whatever,' she murmured, reaching the square of polished tiles, and turning into his arms. 'Don't be a spoil-sport, darling. Don't you want to dance with me?'

Cole scowled, but there was no turning back. Besides, the face she turned up to his was innocent of all deceit, the amber eyes pleading with him to give in.

And he did. With a grim tightening of his lips, he gripped her waist, and held her away from him. Then, fixing his gaze on some distant point above her head, he began to move rather awkwardly in time to the music.

Joanna caught her lower lip between her teeth, as a smile tugged at the corners of her mouth. Oh, lord, she gulped, trying to contain her mirth, she had forgotten what a hopeless dancer Cole was. He had never mastered any step, beyond the square dances he had learned in school, and only her guidance had made him half decent on a dance-floor.

But not like this, she conceded drily, with at least six inches between them. She didn't want to remember the other occasions when they had danced together, but she couldn't help it. Then, the steps they used hadn't been important. They had moved to the rhythm of their bodies—just like when they were making love...

She shivered, and the feathering of her flesh reminded her of where she was, and what she was doing. The dance-floor was getting crowded, and when a careless elbow nudged her in the ribs her determination hardened. She could have withstood the painful jab quite easily, but she chose not to. With a startled cry, she launched herself against him, successfully dislodging his hands, and clutching his lapels.

'God!'

Cole's reaction was just as violent as she had anticipated, but when he would have drawn back again her hands slid up to his neck.

'Sorry,' she breathed, her breath wafting sweetly across his cheek, and a nerve jerked spasmodically at his jawline.

'What in hell do you think you're doing?' he demanded, his hands reaching up to grab her forearms, with the obvious intention of hauling them down from his shoulders. 'Damn you, keep still!'

'I'm just dancing,' she protested innocently, rotating her hips against his. 'Don't be so touchy! You need all the help you can get.'

'I did warn you,' he grated, and with a little sigh Joanna allowed him to pull her arms down to her sides.

But she didn't move away from him. And, although Cole would clearly have preferred to leave the dance-floor, they were trapped within the circle of the other dancers.

'Is this so bad?' she asked, looking up at him with wide tawny eyes, and she saw the glittering awareness enter his. He might not want to admit it, but his reasons for keeping her at a distance were not because he didn't like dancing with her. And when his gaze dropped to the appealing curve of her soft mouth Joanna felt her own senses sharpen.

'We're leaving,' said Cole abruptly, taking her upper arm between his forefinger and thumb, and pushing her determinedly through the swaying press of people. His nails bit into her flesh as he steered her back to their table. 'Get your bag. I'll pay the bill.'

'But what about our coffee?' she argued, looking longingly at the breakfast-size cups of the aromatic brew waiting on the table, but Cole was unrepentant.

'You can get some coffee back at the hotel,' he stated bleakly, and summoned the startled waiter who had served them.

Outside, Joanna did feel slightly unsteady in the night air. But Cole's expression forbade any attempt to use his arm for support, and when the taxi came she collapsed gratefully into the back.

Cole gave the driver his instructions, and then joined her on the back seat. But his mouth was scornful in the half-light. 'You really are smashed, aren't you?' he declared, shaking his head. 'My God! And I thought we might have a serious conversation.'

Joanna turned her head towards him, her dark hair falling sensuously over one shoulder. 'What about?' she asked silkily, sweeping it back again. 'The fact that you still want me?'

Cole swore, and turned his head away. 'You wish,' he snarled, clenching his fists. 'God, why did I ever agree to this pointless exercise?'

'Because Daddy asked you to,' retorted Joanna shortly. 'And you always do everything Daddy says, don't you? You're Daddy's blue-eyed boy. Even if it means sacrificing other people in the process!'

Cole's jaw clamped. 'Shut up!'

'Why?' Joanna felt fairly safe in baiting him, with the comfortingly broad shoulders of the Bahamian taxi driver firmly in view. 'You don't like to hear the truth, Cole. In fact, you don't hear anything but what Daddy says. I'm surprised you ever learned how to have sex with a woman! Or was Daddy in on that, too——?'

Cole moved then, covering the space between them in one swift lunge. His hand closed about her throat, cutting off her words with unexpected violence, and his eyes glittered dangerously in the twilight world of the cab.

'Shut up,' he commanded again. 'Shut the hell up!' And then, as her eyes fought with his, and terror gripped her stomach, he uttered a muffled oath and brought his mouth down on hers.

As kisses went, it wasn't pleasant. With Cole's hand practically cutting off the air to her windpipe, Joanna could hardly have been expected to enjoy it. On top of that, despite the lightness of his hair, and the fact that he had probably shaved before coming out, Cole's chin was abrasively male. And as his mouth ground against her teeth, all Joanna could think of was how abused she was going to look when he let go of her.

But something happened when he kissed her. Although his original intention had been to hurt and humiliate her, that melding of their mouths seduced his reason. A groan of anguish rumbled in his throat, and he tore his mouth from hers, only to return again with an urgent imprecation.

And when he did so, his fingers relaxed, releasing her throat from his throttling grasp. Instead of bruising her flesh, they became achingly gentle, smoothing the tortured skin with a sensuous caress.

Now, Joanna felt as if her breathing had been suspended. Her chest rose and fell with the tumult of her emotions, but she didn't seem to be getting any oxygen into her lungs. Indeed, there didn't seem to be enough oxygen in the car, and her senses swam dizzily beneath his searching touch.

Cole's kiss became hungry, and fiercely demanding. His tongue forced its way into her mouth, and she let it have its way. That hot, wet invader was disturbingly familiar, and her tongue twined around it, helpless to resist. There was nothing gentle about him now, but his demands inspired a matching need. Her legs splayed, her head dipped low against the squabs, and when his hand slid inside the neckline of her dress and touched her breasts she felt her arousal, clear down to her thighs.

The cab, braking outside the brilliantly lit foyer of the Coral Bay Hotel, brought Cole, belatedly, to his senses. With a groan of anguish he pushed himself up and away from her, but not before the smirking taxi driver had glimpsed what had been going on.

Joanna struggled up with rather less energy. She was still bemused by the upheaval of her senses, and it was difficult to think coherently, when her body was dewy with perspiration. Her hair was mussed about her shoulders, and even in the semi-gloom of the cab she guessed her swollen lips had not gone unremarked. And even Cole made a point of buttoning his jacket as he got out of the car.

She knew why, thought Joanna tensely, stumbling out after him. Standing on the floodlit forecourt, she wet her bruised lips with a soothing tongue. Cole had been as aroused as she was. She had felt the heavy heat of his manhood against her stomach, its throbbing tumescence straining at the zip of his trousers. Known, too, that Cole's self-control had been slipping. He had wanted her; she knew it. And if they hadn't been interrupted...

'Let's get inside.'

Cole's hand at her elbow, and his harsh impersonal tone brought her swiftly back to earth. With a gesture that was barely civil, he escorted her inside the hotel. Then, after accompanying her to the bank of elevators, he inclined his head and released her.

But, when he would have walked away, Joanna caught his arm. 'Where are you going?'

Cole's eyes flickered over her flushed face, which still bore the signs of his assault, but there was no compassion in his gaze. 'I need a drink,' he replied, removing her hand from his sleeve. 'Go to bed. You're a mess!'

Joanna winced at his callous choice of words, but she didn't let him see he had hurt her. 'And if I am?' she taunted. 'Whose fault is that? What's the matter, Cole? Don't you like seeing the proof of your weakness?'

'Damn you,' he said, but she guessed his choice of epithet was for other ears than her own. If they had been alone, he would not have been so polite. She could think of other—four-letter—words he had used with less provocation. 'I don't want to see you again,' he added, his mouth curling contemptuously. 'I'll be leaving in the morning. If you have any sense, you'll stay out of my way till then.'

Joanna held up her head. 'All right,' she said. 'If that's what you want.' And afterwards she bitterly regretted the need to thwart him that had taken over her already battered ego. 'But don't you think you ought to tell me what time we're leaving? I've got to pack and pay my bill. And I'd like to phone Grace, and my parents, just to let them know what I'm doing.'

In her room, some time later, Joanna was still appalled at the predicament her impulsive tongue had got her into. My God, she thought, as if she couldn't just have been grateful that Cole was leaving, without achieving what he had come here to do! He had already been as mad as hell. She knew that. He would have liked nothing better than to slam his fist into her face for the crazy way he had acted in the taxi. But no. Just because he had chosen to vent some of his spleen on her, she had retaliated in the most asinine way imaginable. She had actually agreed to do the very thing she had sworn she would never do: go back to Tidewater.

She was so stupid, she groaned now, flinging off the satin sheath, and marching into the bathroom. She had got her way, and she had fluffed it. She had completely screwed up. Instead of waving Cole a mocking farewell, she had agreed to go with him. She couldn't back out now without losing all her credibility.

And, although Cole had been incensed by her announcement tonight, that had only been his knee-jerk reaction. Sooner or later, he was going to realise exactly what it meant. He had got his own way, without any further effort on his part.

A cold shower later, Joanna was still in no state to try and get some sleep. Besides, she supposed she ought to make some attempt at her packing. Although Cole had refused to discuss his travel arrangements with her, a swift call to the hotel concierge had elicited the information that the Charleston flight left at eleven-thirty the next morning. That meant leaving for the airport soon after nine, which would leave her very little time for organising her affairs. Of course, what the concierge had not been able to tell her was whether there were any seats available on the flight. The airline offices were closed for the night, so that would have to wait. But, one way or another, she was committed to making the effort. And if the flight was full, there would be others.

Groaning, she flopped down on to the side of her bed, hitching up the towel, which was her only covering. She needed to talk to somebody, she thought unhappily. Preferably, someone who wouldn't tell her she was all kinds of an idiot for getting herself into this mess. There only was one person: Grace.

Picking up the phone, she dialled for an outside line, and when the dial tone came through she punched in Grace's London number. It seemed to ring forever, and she was on the point of replacing the receiver when Grace picked up the phone.

'Yes?' she said, and there was a lazily peeved edge to her voice. 'Who's there?'

'Me. Jo. Joanna,' she responded uncharitably. 'Where were you?'

'Try bed,' retorted Grace shortly. And then, 'Jo, do you have any idea what time it is here?'

'Oh, lord!' Joanna pushed back her damp hair with a guilty hand. 'Oh, hell, Grace, I'm sorry. I never thought——'

'Obviously.' But Grace's impatience was giving way to anxiety now. 'So, what is it? What's wrong?'

'Oh, Grace!' Joanna sighed. 'Look, it's not that important. I'll talk to you tomorrow——'

'Don't you dare!' Grace said something in a muffled aside—to Ray, Joanna suspected, feeling even worse—and then continued forcefully, 'Come on, Jo. Spit it out. It's Cole, isn't it? What's happened? Has he been threatening you?'

If only, thought Joanna ruefully, flinging herself back on the bed. His threats she could deal with. It was his frustration she found so appealing.

'No,' she replied now, examining the fingernails of one hand, in an effort to sustain normality. 'No, he hasn't been threatening me, Grace.' She paused, and then added painfully, 'I've said I'll go with him.'

'To Tidewater?'

Grace was evidently astounded, and Joanna couldn't blame her after what she had said. But, 'Yes,' she agreed, finding it no easier to cope with now than she had earlier. 'So tell me how I can get out of it, without looking a complete idiot.'

'But, Jo, you said——'

'I know what I said, Grace. But—well, Cole made me mad, and I just said the first thing that came into my head.'

'That you'd go to Tidewater?'

'Yes.'

'But why?'

It was obvious that Grace couldn't comprehend her reasoning, and without any explanation of the facts Joanna could understand her bewilderment. But how could she tell Grace what had happened in the taxi? How could she explain what Cole had done? In retrospect, it all seemed slightly incredible anyway, even to her.

'He—said something,' she mumbled now, half wishing she had never made this call. But she hadn't known that Ray Marsden would still be there. From what Grace had told her in the past, she had assumed their relationship was still fairly perfunctory. But, if Ray was sleeping at the gallery...

'Something rather important, by the sound of it,' Grace put in drily, when Joanna said nothing more. 'I take it you've not had second thoughts?'

'About his father?' Joanna's lips tightened. 'No.'

'I see.' Grace sounded troubled. And then, to her companion, 'Tea? Oh, yes, darling, that would be lovely.'

Joanna pushed herself up again. 'I'd better go——'

'You'd better not.' Grace snorted. 'OK. Ray's gone to get us some tea, bless him. So, why don't you tell me what this is really all about?'

Joanna caught her breath. 'I've told you——'

'That you're going back with Cole? Yes, I know. But what did he say, for God's sake? And why would anything he said persuade you? You seemed so—adamant!'

'I was. I *am*.' Joanna hunched her shoulders. 'Oh—well, if you must know, he—he made a pass at me.' A *pass*? Liar!

'He made a pass at you?' Grace was clearly flabbergasted. 'When? Where?'

Joanna licked her dry lips. 'He—took me out for dinner.'

'Last night?'

'Well, tonight, actually,' murmured Joanna ruefully. 'It's only eleven o'clock here.'

'Of course.' Grace gave a resigned sigh. 'So where is he now?'

'Where is he?' Joanna frowned. 'What do you mean, where is he? He's in his room, I suppose. Probably fast asleep by now.'

'Hmm.' Grace hesitated. 'Well, I hope you haven't done anything stupid!'

Joanna blinked. 'Anything stupid?' she echoed. 'Don't you call agreeing to go back to Tidewater stupid?'

'You know what I mean, Jo.'

'No, I'm afraid I don't.' Joanna was totally confused. 'Are we talking at cross purposes here?'

Grace groaned. 'Jo, what I'm asking is, are you still taking the pill?'

'The pill?' For a beat, Grace's meaning was lost to her. 'What pill?'

'*The* pill,' exclaimed Grace, not without some impatience. 'For pity's sake, Jo, you know what kind of pill I'm talking about.'

'Oh!' Joanna felt the hot colour run up her face, and was glad no one else could see it. '*That* pill.' She swallowed. 'Well, no, of course not.'

'*Jo!*'

Joanna gasped. 'I haven't had sex with him, Grace!' She shook her head. 'What do you take me for?'

'Well, thank heavens for that.' Grace sounded distinctly relieved. 'When you said——'

'When I said Cole made a pass at me, I didn't mean we'd been to bed together.' Joanna was indignant.

'So why are you so upset?'

'I should have thought that was obvious.'

'Because you've said you'll go with him?'

'That's right.'

'Was that before or after he made a pass at you?'

'After, of course.'

'Why, of course?' Grace sounded sardonic. 'Jo, if you were upset because Cole—well, because of what he did—why on earth did you tell him you'd go with him?'

'Because it made him mad!' retorted Joanna crossly. 'He—resented the fact that he still—well, that I could still——'

'I get the picture.' Grace's tone was dry. 'Well, love, I don't see how you can back out now. Not unless you want Cole to think you're afraid of him. But, please— be careful. I don't think you realise how vulnerable you are.'

CHAPTER FIVE

JOANNA had heard Charleston compared to an eighteenth-century Venice, and from the air that description seemed even more apt. With its old but elegant houses, painted white and gleaming in the sun, it had an indomitable air. As it stood on a peninsula, with the sea never far from its back door, it was not surprising that its real heyday had been in the latter years of the eighteenth century, when the great sailing fleets from Europe had followed the trade winds to the Caribbean. Twentieth-century Charleston was rather less successful, but its jumbled streets and ante-bellum colonialism were preserved here as nowhere else.

Not that Joanna knew the city very well. In the early days of their marriage, Cole had shown her the tourists' view of Charleston, and the military academy, and the curved esplanade, known as the Battery, were fairly familiar to her. But Tidewater Plantation was some distance from the city, and the small town of Beaumaris was their main supplier.

None the less, it had given her her first taste of South Carolina, and she could still remember the heat and the humidity, and the rain, which had come in a bone-chilling deluge. But she hadn't cared in those days. She was in love with Cole, and she would have lived in the heart of a volcano, if he had asked her to.

How foolish she had been, she thought now, turning her head to look at her antagonist, lounging carelessly in the seat beside her. How naïve! In those days life had seemed so simple, so uncomplicated. She had actually believed in happy-ever-after. But that was before she had met Cole's family, and realised that, so far as they were concerned, Cole had made a terrible mistake. In marrying her, of course, she appended harshly. Macallisters did not marry outsiders, particularly not women, who had too much to say for themselves.

Joanna sighed. She hadn't considered she was particularly opinionated before she went to live in Tidewater County. Nor especially revolutionary either, until Ryan Macallister put her straight. Macallisters didn't mix with the poorer families of the district. They didn't set up maternity clinics, or treat the plantation workers as social equals. Not openly, anyway. The fact that Ryan Macallister promulgated one policy, and practised another, was what had brought Joanna into open conflict with her father-in-law. And signalled the end of her marriage, she acknowledged bitterly. That . . . and Nathan's death . . .

But she didn't want to think about Nathan now. The pain of that tragedy, and the ugly lies that had caused it, didn't hurt her any more. Not a lot, anyway. Time had laid its healing balm over those old wounds, and she would be unwise to test its resistance. It was enough that Cole had proved he was not immune to the past, and it was going to be amusing showing his father exactly how futile his schemes had been.

Or would it? Joanna chewed unhappily at her lower lip. She was not naturally a vindictive woman, and the unwilling memory of why she was here brought its own uncertainty. How could she stand up to a man who was already dying? What crueller retribution could there be? And she still had to find out why he should want to see her. As far as she was aware, they had nothing more to say to one another.

The stewardess's warning, to take note of the 'Fasten Seatbelts' sign, and to extinguish all cigarettes, reminded her of the imminence of their arrival. Checking that her seatbelt was securely in place, Joanna's eyes briefly locked with Cole's. But she could read nothing from his expression and, in any case, he looked away. As he had done since this morning, when they had shared a cab to the airport on New Providence. He had made it blatantly obvious that he had decided to remove himself mentally, if not physically, from any contact between them, and, for the time being, Joanna was prepared to let him.

That they were travelling together at all was another matter. Joanna had felt justifiably furious when she woke up that morning, and found the plane reservation that had been pushed under her door. She had not slept particularly well, and, snatching up the folder, she had discovered, to her chagrin, that the booking had been made the previous day. It was galling to think that, even after all she had said, Cole had been so sure of her compliance. As soon as she accepted his dinner invitation, he must have thought it was a foregone conclusion. The only comfort she had was that the evening had not gone exactly as he had planned. He might have got his own way, but at what cost to his self-esteem?

An hour later, Joanna was already feeling the effects of the pre-summer heat in this semi-tropical corner of the United States. Cole's brother, Ben, had met them at the airport. After a rather awkward greeting, he had loaded Cole's flight bag and her own suitcases into the back of the solid four-by-four estate car, before taking the wheel for the drive to Tidewater. He had been polite, but hardly friendly, and as Cole had been eager to hear about their father they had immediately excluded her from their easy communication.

Not that she cared, thought Joanna, not altogether honestly. Just because she and Ben had once been friends was no reason to feel slighted now. It was obvious that he would take his brother's—and his father's—word before her own. And she had no doubt her name had figured in some bitter conversations.

But, for now, she contained her feelings, and fanned herself with a languid hand. Although she was almost sure the vehicle possessed an air-conditioning system, Ben was driving along the coastal highway with all the windows open. In consequence, the moist air was causing her shirt and cotton cut-offs to cling to her damp body, and it was enough to try and find a comfortable position. Nevertheless, she viewed the back of Cole's head with some resentment. He was on his own ground here, and the heat didn't bother him a scrap.

Yet, for all her frustration, Joanna couldn't deny the attraction of the area. Humid it might be, but it was also lush, and colourful, and extremely beautiful. The coastal region was a mass of lakes and waterways, where salt marshes melted into acres of sand dunes, and houses were built high for coolness. At this time of the year, gardens were alight with crimson and pink azaleas, blooming amid jasmine and roses, waxy white camellias and flowering dogwood. Wistaria overhung walls and porches, and wide verandas sported terracotta tubs, and cane furniture. This was the low country, and life moved at a less hectic pace than in the city.

Deciding she wasn't prepared to be ignored for the whole journey, Joanna unfastened another button on her shirt, and determinedly leaned forward. Resting her arms along the backs of the seats in front, she expelled a sigh that just happened to waft close to Cole's ear, and forced a smile.

'So—how are you, Ben?' she enquired, ignoring Cole's sudden intake of breath. 'Got your own place yet?'

'Um——' Ben cast a worried look in Cole's direction, before shaking his head. 'N-no. Not yet. Too much to do around Tidewater.'

Joanna's lips flattened. 'But I thought you wanted a place of your own,' she persisted, and Cole turned his head to give her a dark look. 'Well, he did,' she added, responding to that grim warning. 'How old are you now, Ben? Twenty-five? Twenty-six?'

'He's twenty-four,' stated her ex-husband shortly. 'Two years younger than you, as I'm sure you know very well.'

'You remembered!' Joanna's brows arched with teasing intent. 'That makes you thirty, doesn't it?' She tugged the neckline of the shirt away from her moist throat. 'My, aren't we getting old?'

Cole didn't dignify her remark with a reply. He merely swung round in his seat again, leaving Joanna to search wildly for something else to say. But she had no intention of letting him intimidate her, verbally or otherwise, and when her elbow brushed his neck she was more than satisfied by his sharp withdrawal.

'Cole tells me Joe's married now,' she inserted, into a conversation about the current state of land erosion. She had addressed her question to Ben again, and, once more, he looked at his older brother before replying.

' 'S right,' he muttered, clearly not enjoying being pig-in-the-middle, but Joanna couldn't afford to consider anyone's feelings but her own.

'And he still lives at home?' she prompted. 'It's just as well it's a big house. With three families living in it.'

Now Ben glanced at her. '*Three* families?'

Joanna nodded. 'Well, as Cole and Joe both have wives——'

'Cole doesn't——' he began impulsively, and then he broke off, his fair skin suffused with colour. 'That is——' He swallowed convulsively, his Adam's apple protruding through his taut skin, and he gave his brother a sidelong look. 'Didn't Cole tell you?'

'Obviously not.' Cole spoke before Joanna could say anything else to embarrass him. He looked at her now, but his blue eyes were as cold as glaciers. 'Sammy-Jean left Tidewater some time ago,' he told her bleakly. 'She lives in California, as far as I know. Does that satisfy you?'

It didn't, but Joanna was too surprised to say anything at that moment. No, more than that, she admitted. She was shocked. Astounded. After all, Sammy-Jean had been Ryan Macallister's choice of a wife for his eldest son. And Joanna knew the other woman had been after Cole ever since they were in high school together. She had made no secret of it. She had been crazy about him. And crazy for him. So what had gone wrong?

With her mind already probing the implications of this announcement, the obvious question sprang to her lips. 'Are—are you divorced?'

Cole's exhalation of breath was savage. 'Yes,' he said curtly. 'Now can we leave it? It's no concern of yours.'

Wasn't it? Joanna wondered. Would she have come here at all, if she had known Sammy-Jean wasn't going to be around to protect her? She wasn't prepared to consider at this moment why she should think she needed any protection. Suffice it to say that Grace's final words suddenly had a deeper meaning.

'Does—does Grace know?'

She had to ask, and Cole uttered an aggravated oath. 'I said we wouldn't talk about it.'

'No, but——'

'God!' He raked angry fingers against his scalp. 'What does it matter?' And then, after allowing himself a minute to calm down, he added, 'Of course she knows. Why wouldn't she? It's not a secret, for God's sake.'

'Then why didn't she tell me?' demanded Joanna, and then wished she hadn't, when sardonic eyes were turned in her direction.

'Who knows?' taunted Cole, enjoying her discomfort. 'Perhaps she was afraid you might come rushing back to comfort me.'

Joanna's hands clenched on the leather back of the wide seats, but, although her initial reaction was to retaliate in kind, this time she thought before she spoke. 'Perhaps I would at that,' she murmured, aware that Ben's head had swung round at her words. He was obviously bewildered by the sudden switch in emphasis, and he showed it. 'Did you need comforting?'

'Not by you,' declared Cole rudely, salvaging what he could from the wreckage. 'When I need a woman, I can always pay for one.'

'Just like your daddy,' retorted Joanna, stung in spite of herself.

Flinging herself back in the seat then, she tried to ignore the sudden pain his words had brought her. It was all very well trading insults with him, but for all her determination her skin was not as thick as his. She scowled sourly out of the window. Bastard, she thought, finding some relief in calling him names, even if he couldn't hear. Jerk! Creep! How could she have allowed herself to get into this situation?

They passed the exit for Beaumaris, and the sign that read 'You are now entering Tidewater County', but Joanna hardly noticed. She was too wrapped up in feelings of bitterness and frustration, and it wasn't until they turned between the gates of Tidewater Plantation that a sense of panic gripped her stomach. They were here, she gagged. They were really here. Tidewater! Where she had sworn she would never set foot again.

She tried to calm herself. Arriving at the house in a state of wild emotion would get her nowhere. She needed every bit of self-confidence she possessed to face Cole's family. Not to mention a stiff back and a strong will, she added grimly. No one was going to make a fool of her again.

They approached the house through an avenue of live oaks liberally hung with Spanish moss. The creeper gave the trees an eerie, ghostlike appearance, particularly at night, when dampness rose from the river to cloak the house in a drifting grey mist. At other times, with the moon shining through the swaying tendrils, it could be quite romantic, and Joanna found herself remembering the first night she had spent here, when Cole had taken her to see the river, and they had made love on a bed of wild thyme...

She expelled a harsh breath, and hauled herself up in the seat. Now was not the time to start remember-

ing things like that, she chided herself grimly. She had
been incredibly foolish in those days. She had actually
believed that love could conquer all. How stupid could
you get?

Forcing herself to look around, Joanna cast a detached eye over the lush paddocks that lay beyond the
white fence that edged the driveway. Glossy-coated
mares, and their foals, cropped acres of green, green
grass, and the breeze that invaded the windows of the
car came straight from the salt marshes. She knew it
was possible to see the ocean from the first-floor balcony of the house, and with the river lapping not too
far from its doors you were never far from the sight
and sound of water.

But, although Tidewater had not yet succumbed to
the lure of turning itself into a tourist attraction, as so
many other plantations had done, it no longer relied on
its cultivation of rice and indigo to keep it solvent.
Nowadays, many of the rice fields had been drained,
and given over to the raising of cattle, and thorough-
bred horses lived in stables that had once quartered its
immigrant work-force.

Not that Joanna had taken any part in the running
of the estate. As Cole's wife, she had been entitled to
live in the house, and eat at the table, but anything
more than that had been denied to her. Ryan
Macallister and his sons ran the plantation, and his
wife ran the house. And Margaret Macallister had
wanted no help from anyone, least of all a girl her son
had married against their wishes.

A shiver feathered along Joanna's spine. Now that
she was here, so many memories came flooding back
to her. How could she have forgotten the many humil-
iations she had suffered at Cole's mother's hands—the

petty slights and ignominies that Cole had known nothing about?

She caught her lower lip between her teeth as she remembered. She had come from a normal, loving family, a family that had welcomed Cole into their midst with no real reservations. Even though it had meant Joanna leaving her home, and her country, to go and live in some distant corner of the New World, her parents had accepted it. They had accepted that she loved Cole, and he loved her, and that she knew what she was doing. They had granted her the privilege of believing her old enough to make her own decisions, and although they were going to miss her terribly they had been generous in their support.

Not so Cole's family. From the beginning, Joanna had been left in no doubt as to their disapproval of the marriage, and, although in those early days Cole had defended her against any overt criticism, when he wasn't there she was vulnerable. The truth was, she had never encountered that kind of antagonism before, and Margaret Macallister had lost no opportunity to belittle her in front of her husband.

It still hurt. Tamping down the choking sense of indignation that rose in her throat, Joanna forced herself to remember that this time it was going to be different. She hadn't wanted to come here; they had sent for her. And she was an independent woman now, not a lovesick girl, with no experience of life.

She could just imagine how her mother would react, when she found out where her daughter had gone. That was why she had prevailed on Grace to ring her parents and tell them what she was doing. She had known that, if she had spoken to her mother, Mrs Seton would have done her utmost to get her to change her mind. And, for all her determination, Joanna had not been sufficiently confident of her own ability to withstand such an onslaught.

Now, as they approached the house, Joanna began to wonder if it wouldn't have been more sensible to get her mother's opinion. Maybe she was making a terrible mistake.

But the sound of barking dogs and the slowing of the estate car made such misgivings immaterial. A bend in the drive had revealed the house, standing squarely against a backdrop of oak and pine trees. Its white-painted walls and verandas stretched majestically towards a sky splashed with the colours of early evening, and Joanna's nerves prickled in anticipation. Grills, lattices, louvred shutters; it had all the elegance of a bygone era. And, although the original plantation house had long since fallen into decay, this outward facsimile, built between the two great wars, was every bit as imposing as its antecedent.

Joanna stiffened. Just seeing the house, and the handful of foxhounds that rushed excitedly to meet the car, brought an unwelcome feeling of *déjà vu*. Only it had been old Moses, one of the grooms, who had met her and Cole on that first occasion. A warning of the opposition they had had to face.

The big Buick came to a halt, and Cole had his door open almost before the wheels had stopped turning. Ordering the hounds away, he turned to open Joanna's door, just as a tall, well-built woman emerged from the house.

Joanna's stomach hollowed. Margaret—Maggie—Macallister hadn't changed. She was still as formidable as ever, her broad-shouldered figure clad in one of

the floral prints she favoured, and her long grey hair
wound in a plaited coronet around her head.

'Cole,' she said, in a voice that was half accusing,
half relieved, 'thank God you're home!'

'Why?' Leaving Joanna's door ajar, Cole sprang up
the flight of steps to where his mother was waiting on
the veranda. 'Nothing's happened, has it? Pa's
not——'

'No, no. He's the same.' Gripping her eldest son by
the shoulders, Maggie Macallister looked at him with
tears glistening in her eyes. 'I was just—so worried.
When you didn't come back yesterday——?'

She didn't finish the sentence, but Joanna, climbing
reluctantly out of the car, thought its meaning was unmistakable. Cole's mother was reminding him of his
responsibilities, and using the opportunity to show her
exactly what to expect.

'I'm sorry.' Cole allowed his mother to pull him into
an eager embrace, and Joanna, hauling out a heavy
suitcase and her flight bag, couldn't help but glimpse
the look of triumph Maggie Macallister cast in her direction. You might have seduced him away from his
family once, that look seemed to say, but, as you can
see, it won't happen again.

Won't it? thought Joanna grimly, tugging at the
second suitcase. We'll see, you old harridan! We'll see
who has the last laugh!

'Here—I'll do that.'

Joanna was so intent on giving back stare for stare
that she had been unaware of Ben coming round the
vehicle to help her.

'Let me,' he insisted, lifting the second case effort-
lessly on to the crushed-shell forecourt, and Joanna

gave him a winning smile that was all the warmer because of its audience.

'Thanks,' she said, deliberately tipping her head to one side, and looking him over. 'I'd forgotten you were so strong.' She touched his biceps with teasing fingers. 'Solid muscle!'

'And no brains,' said Cole abruptly, pulling himself out of his mother's arms, and coming back down the steps to where Ben was red-facedly trying to handle all the luggage. He gave Joanna a chilling look, and took one of the cases from Ben. 'Come on. I'll show you your room.'

But not without meeting Ma, brooded Joanna unwillingly, following him up the steps. No one was allowed to do anything around here without Ma's permission. And right now Maggie Macallister was watching their exchange with grim-eyed disapproval.

Joanna started to pluck her shirt away from her body as she followed Cole up to where his mother was waiting, but then she changed her mind. What did she care if Maggie Macallister thought she was brazen, because the damp material was clinging to her taut breasts? They were nice breasts—and Ben had evidently thought so, too—judging by the way his eyes had nearly popped out of his head.

Even so, it took an enormous amount of courage to face the woman who had helped to destroy her marriage. For all her resolution, it wasn't easy to forget the last time she had stood on this veranda. Or dismiss the pain and anguish that she would always associate with her departure.

Nevertheless, there was a difference. As Joanna mounted the last stair and came up beside Cole, she realised what it was. Whereas before she had been eager—fool that she was—to make a good impression, now she didn't have to. It didn't matter to her what Cole's mother thought, and although she didn't actually voice the words she saw the dawning comprehension in Maggie Macallister's eyes.

There was an awkward moment, while the two women appeared to size one another up. And then, when it became apparent that her erstwhile daughter-in-law was not going to be the first to speak, Cole's mother cracked a frosty smile.

'Joanna,' she said, regarding the younger woman's appearance with undisguised disdain. 'You look hot.'

'Oh, I am.' Joanna expelled her breath in an upward draught. 'I can't wait to strip off these tight trousers.'

Maggie's mouth compressed. 'I'm sure,' she murmured, exchanging a speaking look with Cole. 'If you wait a moment, I'll get Sally to show you to your room.'

'Oh, but...' Joanna pretended a confusion she certainly wasn't feeling. 'Cole said he'd show me where I'm to sleep.' Her look was all wide-eyed innocence. 'Isn't that right, honey?'

It was hard to decide who was the most incensed by her remark, but Cole recovered first. 'That's right,' he said tersely, picking up her cases again, and making for the open doorway. 'We don't want there to be any mistake, do we?'

'Hell, no.' Before Maggie could make any endorsing statement, Joanna pulled a rueful face. 'I might find myself sharing a bathroom with you, sugar.'

'Unlikely,' the older woman assured her coldly, having no choice but to follow them into the house. 'I

don't think any of us is likely to forget the past,
Joanna. Least of all Cole.'

Joanna's jaw compressed, but, try as she might, she
couldn't think of any flip comment to make. And while
she was in that state of uncertainty Cole's elbow
nudged her in the back.

'Let's go,' he said, jerking his head towards the
forked staircase that led up to a galleried landing. 'Before I'm tempted to put a foot in that big mouth of
yours.'

CHAPTER SIX

JOANNA lingered in the shower, resting her slim back against the cold tiled wall, and allowing the pummelling spray to do its worst. But it was so good to feel cool again, and she was loath to step out into the moist evening air.

Beyond her windows, the velvety darkness was alive with the whirrings and rustlings of the night. Huge moths beat their wings against her blinds, and she'd already had to dispose of a family of termites that had taken up residence on her veranda. She'd forgotten how many minor drawbacks there were to living at Tidewater, and her city sensibilities needed to be redefined.

But she had wanted to call for help when she found a cockroach in the shower-stall. She hated the ugly insects, with their hard shells, that crunched if you stood on them. Nevertheless, she had dealt with it herself. After the harsh words she and Cole had exchanged, she doubted he would have been willing to accommodate her. And, although she could have summoned one of the servants to attend to it, she was unwilling to show any softness in this house.

Besides, she wasn't usually so squeamish. It was just that it had been a long day, and these small difficulties were wearing away her defences. She needed time to adjust—to adapt to her situation, and restore her equilibrium. But, if Cole had his way, she wasn't going to get it. In fifteen minutes, she was expected to go downstairs and join the family for the evening meal.

Pushing herself away from the wall, she reached out and turned off the taps. Then, sweeping the curtain aside, she stepped out on to the marble-tiled floor. A huge white bathsheet encased her from her neck to her ankles, and, draping it securely about her, she padded through to the bedroom.

Viewing her appearance in the gilt-edged pier-glass, she felt a sense of resignation. Her haunted expression was not what she wanted to see, and the stark whiteness of the towel accentuated the dark rings around her eyes. She looked—defeated, she thought impatiently. Young, and vulnerable, and—defeated. And all because she was hot, and tired, and desperate to see a friendly face.

The knock that came at her door at that moment was badly timed. At the sound, all her defences sprang into active life, and with her hackles up, and her hands clenched tightly in the folds of the towel, she determined not to answer it.

But when the door-handle rattled she tensed in dismay. There had been no key to lock the door, and although she had wedged the back of the chair beneath the handle before she went for her shower she doubted it would be sufficient deterrent to so determined a visitor.

Then she heard someone say her name, and her misgivings fled. The voice was unmistakably feminine, and when the word was repeated in hushed, urgent tones she flew across the room to remove the chair.

She practically flung open the door, and the girl, who had been inclined towards the panels outside, almost fell into the room. 'Jo,' she said again, her face flushed with anxious colour. 'Oh, Jo, I can't believe it!'

'Charley!' Securing the towel beneath her breasts, Joanna withstood the onslaught as Cole's fifteen-year-old sister launched herself at her. 'Gosh, Charley, it's good to see you.'

'You, too.' Charley hugged her with all the strength of her sturdy young frame, and then drew back to gaze at Joanna with unconcealed delight. 'How long are you staying?'

'I—I'm not sure.' Joanna realised that that was something she hadn't given a lot of thought to. 'A few days, maybe.' She blinked back an errant tear. 'So—how are you? And Donna? And Sandy? I guess he must be twelve now, is that right? Heavens, aren't you growing up!'

'We're OK.' Charley gave a careless shrug of her shoulders. She brushed back the thick braid, which was several shades darker than Cole's hair, and grimaced. 'Donna's still Donna, and Sandy still follows Cole around, like he always did.'

Joanna nodded. Donna was Charley's twin, but the two sisters had never been really close. Meanwhile Sandy—Alexander—was the youngest member of the family.

'I guess you know about Pa,' Charley continued now, as Joanna cast a doubtful glance up and down the corridor outside before closing the door. The girl sauntered across the room, evidently dressed for supper, in her white linen tunic, ankle socks, and patent shoes, and picked up Joanna's hairbrush from the dressing-table. 'He's pretty sick.'

'Yes.' Joanna's mouth dried, and she hitched the towel a little tighter. 'I'm—sorry.'

'Why should you be?' Charley swung round to face her. 'It isn't as if you ever liked him.'

Joanna moistened her lips. 'No,' she conceded evenly. 'He's—not an easy man to like.'

'Tell me about it.' Charley raised her eyes towards the ceiling in a gesture that was surprisingly adult for someone of her age. 'You know he's already told me I've *got* to go to college!'

'Well . . .' Joanna lifted her shoulders. 'That doesn't seem too unreasonable——'

'Not to you, maybe.' Charley tossed her head. 'Jo, I don't want to go to college. Donna's the academic one, not me. I'd just as soon stay here and help Ma.'

Joanna shook her head. 'You may change your mind. I mean, it's a few years yet——'

'I won't.' Charley scowled. 'You don't understand, Jo. I—I—want to get married.'

'Married?' Joanna was astounded, and showed it, and Charley hurried on.

'Yes, married,' she said, clasping her hands together and facing Joanna with a stubborn light in her eyes. 'Next year. When I'm sixteen.'

Joanna caught her lower lip between her teeth. 'You've got someone in mind, I gather.'

'Of course.' Charley looked scornful. 'You remember Billy Fenton, don't you? His mother used to visit the clinic. You helped her——'

'I remember Billy Fenton,' Joanna interrupted quickly, her spirits plummeting. The Fentons were a poor white family who occupied a one-roomed shack on the edge of the estate. Boulevard—*Bull*—Fenton used to be employed in the stables, until his craving for liquor and his employer's patience collided. Ryan Macallister had thrown him out, indifferent to the burdens Bull's being without a job would put on his entire family.

Not that people had blamed Cole's father for what he'd done. It was a well-known fact that Bull was bone idle; that he beat his wife and kids, and that he had set up a whiskey still, somewhere back in the woods. Of course, the police had never found any evidence to convict him with, but the rumours persisted, and so did Bull's drunkenness.

But it was Bull's wife, Susan, Joanna had felt sorry for. Although the girl had been little more than her own age, she had already had seven babies, three of whom had been stillborn. She was a little mouse of a creature, afraid of her brutal husband, yet without the will to leave him. All Joanna had been able to do was give her the means to prevent the yearly pregnancies, and gradually, over a period of months, she had seen the woman regaining her self-respect.

Billy had been her oldest child, and thankfully nothing like his father. Joanna guessed he must be sixteen or seventeen now, and probably quite a hero to someone like Charley. But Charley would probably never have noticed him if she hadn't helped Joanna at the clinic during her school holidays. And, while it was unfair to judge Billy because of his background, Joanna knew there was no way Charley's family would countenance such a liaison.

'Why are you looking like that?' the girl demanded now, evidently sensing something from Joanna's silence that Joanna herself had hoped to conceal. 'You think I'm too young, don't you? Well, I'm not. And no one's going to send me away to college, if I don't want to go.'

Joanna breathed a little more freely. In her concern about Billy's suitability, Charley's age hadn't even come into it. But now she seized on the girl's words with some relief.

'I think it's too soon to be thinking about next year,' she replied carefully. 'Heavens, you could change your mind next week.'

'I won't.' Charley sounded very definite. 'So—will you talk to Cole about it? He never listens to me, but I know he'll listen to you.'

'Cole!' Joanna almost laughed. 'Charley, Cole's hardly likely to listen to anything I have to say.'

'He might.' Charley hunched her shoulders. 'And—and if Pa's dying, Cole's going to be the one to make the decisions around here, isn't he?'

Joanna expelled her breath heavily. 'I—look, Charley, we can't talk now. I've got to get my hair dried, and get dressed for supper. Let—er—let me think about it, OK? Now, off you go. Before your mother starts wondering where you are.'

'All right.' Charley bestowed an impulsive kiss on her cheek, and skipped across to the door. 'I'm so glad you're back, Jo. I just know things are going to work out. You'll see.'

Joanna wished she could feel as optimistic, as she hurriedly dried her hair, and pulled on silk leggings and an over-size shirt that barely skimmed the tops of her thighs. The leggings and shirt were cream, and she slotted the ends of a chunky black belt together, and allowed it to rest loosely on her hips. Glossy hooped earrings swung against her neck, and she let her hair loose, a fall of black silk that framed her delicately arched cheekbones, and dipped into the exposed hollow of her throat.

Of course, she was late. Even without Charley's appearance, she would have been hard-pressed to make it downstairs at the appropriate time. As it was, she had the dubious pleasure of being the last to appear, and although she hadn't intended to make an entrance it turned out that way.

The whole family was waiting for her in the library. Even though it was more than three years since she'd left Tidewater, Joanna had known exactly where she would find them. Even the slightly musty smell of the books was the same. And nine pairs of eyes acknowledged her appearance, mostly alike in their expressions of disapproval.

'I'm sorry,' she said, walking into the room with an air of confidence she was far from feeling. 'I hope I haven't kept you waiting long.'

And it was as she was bestowing an appeasing smile on the room in general that she realised one of the pairs of eyes that had monitored her arrival was Ryan Macallister's. Unlike his son, he wasn't standing, which was why Joanna hadn't noticed him at once. He was seated in a wing-back chair, beside the flower-filled fireplace, and even a passing glance was enough for her to realise that Cole had not been exaggerating when he said his father was very ill. Skeletally thin, Ryan seemed to have shrivelled to a shadow of his former self, and in spite of the heat in the room, which the turning fans only moved around, he was wrapped in a Paisley shawl, with a blanket over his knees.

Joanna was temporarily nonplussed. She didn't know what to say to him. It was obvious something was expected of her, but for a moment she felt incapable of speech. Her eyes flickered uncertainly over the other members of the family. Joe, the brother closest to Cole in age, was there, and she assumed the rather sharp-faced woman at his side must be his wife. Certainly, the woman was regarding her with undisguised hostility—much like her mother-in-law, thought Joanna drily. Of course, Charley's was a friendly face, and even Ben's lips moved in silent approbation. But Donna was too much like her mother to offer any support, and Sandy was too young to count. As for Cole . . .

Joanna's gaze turned from his guarded face to Maggie's. Cole's mother was openly contemptuous, but whether that was for her, or for what she was wearing, she couldn't be sure. It was obvious she didn't conform to the standards set by Maggie and her daughters: crisp shirtwaists and white stockings had never been a part of her wardrobe.

Joanna drew a steadying breath, and, realising it was up to her to show all of them that she could not be intimidated, she approached the old man's chair. 'Mr Macallister,' she said, and her cool English voice rang out loud and clear. She had never progressed beyond calling him *Mr* Macallister, and she saw no reason to change that now. 'How are you?'

Ryan Macallister's mouth compressed. 'How do I look?' he enquired harshly, and Joanna realised he had lost none of his irascibility.

She hesitated. 'Not good,' she said at last, to the concerted sound of several indrawn breaths. 'But I'm sure you already know that.'

Ryan's eyes narrowed. They had once been as blue as his son's, but now they were an indeterminate shade of grey. 'Pretty sure of yourself, aren't you?' he muttered, bony fingers kneading the empty glass in his hand. 'Hope I didn't make a mistake bringing you back

here. I don't want any trouble. Not from you, or anyone else.'

Joanna felt an insane desire to laugh. *He* didn't want
any trouble. Dear God, surely he didn't think she did!

'Why did you ask me to come here, Mr Macallister?'
she enquired politely, but Cole's father was not prepared to make it that easy for her.

'You'll find out,' he said gruffly, and then, holding
out his empty glass to Cole, he muttered, 'Get me another drink, will you? And whatever she wants.'

'Ryan!' As her son moved to do his father's bidding, Maggie took an involuntary step forward. 'Ryan,
you know what the doctor said.'

'Don't I just?' The old man gave her a scornful look.
'What's the matter, Maggie? You heard what Joanna
said. I don't look good. And I sure as hell don't feel
good. So why would I restrict myself to one drink,
when two, or even three, make me feel so much better?'

Maggie's thin lips tightened, and the look she cast in
Joanna's direction was baleful. But, thankfully,
Joanna was able to give her attention to choosing a
drink, and if Cole's expression was no less forbidding,
at least he kept his opinion to himself.

'Just fruit juice, please,' she said, deciding that in
this company it would be wise to keep her wits about
her, and only the faint drawing together of Cole's
brows indicated his reaction to it.

Then, as if at some silent signal from their father, the
other members of the family clustered round her. Joe
unbent sufficiently to deposit a swift kiss on her cheek,
before introducing his wife, Alicia, and even Donna
fingered the smooth, satiny fabric of her shirt, and ex-
pressed a wish that she had one like it.

'You're too fat,' remarked Charley, who had never had any tact, and Donna's resentful eyes turned on her twin.

'Jo used to be fat, too,' she retorted, and Joanna thought how typical it was that she should be made the brunt of their argument.

'That was because she drank too much,' countered Charley, uncaring of Joanna's feelings. 'Pa said so.'

'Pa said a lot of things,' said Ben, in a low voice, stepping between the two sisters. 'That doesn't mean it was true. Now, why don't you two stop embarrassing Jo, and go and help Lacey?'

'Lacey doesn't need any help,' said Charley, but she gave Joanna a rueful smile as she did so. 'Sorry. I didn't mean you used to be really fat. Just—just——'

'Overweight?' suggested Joanna drily, and Charley gave a vigorous nod.

'Clear off,' ordered Ben, not at all appeased by his sister's attempt at an apology, and the twins mooched away, still continuing their argument. 'So,' he added, when they were alone, 'is it as bad as you expected?'

Joanna allowed herself a wry smile. 'Worse?' she suggested lightly, and then shook her head. 'No. Not worse. Different.'

'Because of Pa,' murmured Ben, moving so that he was between her and his father, and Joanna nodded.

'It's funny,' she said, only just realising that it was true. 'He doesn't scare me any more. Why's that, do you suppose?'

'Because he's ill?'

'No.' Joanna frowned. 'At least, I don't think so. He's still as belligerent as ever, and it's obvious he still has all of you running round after him.'

'Except Cole,' said Ben softly, and Joanna looked up at him in surprise.

'What do you mean?'

'You'll find out.' Ben shrugged. 'Cole's changed. He's not the same as he used to be.'

Joanna glanced towards her ex-husband, who was presently making his way towards them, a tall glass of fruit cordial in his hand. 'He seems the same to me,' she muttered, in an undertone, and Ben raised his eyebrows meaningfully as Cole joined them.

'One fruit juice,' he said, handing Joanna the glass, before giving his brother a studied look. 'Did I interrupt something?'

'Heck, no.' Ben coloured a little now, and Joanna's feeling towards him warmed, at this indication of his youth. 'We were just discussing Pa, that's all.'

Cole turned his head to where Joe and Alicia were standing over his father's chair, and then pulled a wry face. 'He seems more animated tonight than I've seen him in a while.' His cool gaze moved to Joanna. 'Perhaps we have you to thank for that.'

'Oh, heaven forbid that you should have to thank me for anything,' Joanna responded mockingly. She tasted her drink, and then put out her tongue to lick the last drop of mango juice from her lips. 'Hmm, this is delightful! I'm glad you made it, Cole. I'm sure your mother wishes it was hemlock!'

'You can't blame my mother for not trusting you,' declared Cole, in a low, harsh tone, and Ben, evidently feeling surplus to requirements, went to stop Sandy from tormenting the twins. 'You didn't exactly make things easy for her.'

'It wasn't my fault that your father's duplicity came home to roost,' responded Joanna shortly, and then, forcing herself not to get involved in another argument with him, she added, 'Is Sarah still living in Beaumaris, by the way? I'd like to see her while I'm here.'

'That's not a good idea,' said Cole, staring at some point over her head. 'I doubt if that was why my father brought you here.'

'I doubt if it was,' agreed Joanna pleasantly. 'But, nevertheless, I intend to see her. With or without your approval.'

Cole's eyes were dark with anger when they dropped to hers again. 'Don't,' he said savagely. 'You'll only cause her more pain. Nathan's dead, and there's nothing any of us can do about it.'

'And aren't you glad?' she retorted, suddenly finding the fruit juice too sweet for her taste. She set down her glass, and looked round for Ben. 'Excuse me; I need some fresh air.'

'Wait!'

Cole's hand around her upper arm arrested her, and even through the material of her shirt she could sense the frustration in those fingers.

'Yes?' She tilted her face up to his, and, although only seconds before she had been goading him with memories of his dead brother, suddenly the air between them fairly crackled with electricity.

'Please,' he said, and she sensed how hard it was for him to plead with her. Her stomach hollowed at the look of stark anguish in his face, and for a moment she would have promised him anything. 'Stay away from Sarah,' he added thickly. 'Stay away, or—or I'll——'

He broke off abruptly, but Joanna had stiffened. 'Or what, Cole?' she taunted, her weakness coagulating into a hard core of resentment inside her. 'You can't threaten me. If I want to see Sarah, I will. Why shouldn't I? We have a lot in common. We both trusted men who betrayed us.' And, lifting his fingers from her sleeve, she walked swiftly away.

'*Jo*!'

His violent use of her name fell on deaf ears, and his mother, who had been watching their altercation with evident misgivings, now came after Joanna.

'Is something wrong?' she demanded, reaching the louvred doors just ahead of her quarry. 'What has Cole been saying?'

Joanna's look of disbelief was not feigned. 'I beg your pardon?'

'I said——'

'I know what you said.' Joanna looked about her with some frustration. 'But I don't think it's any of your business, do you?'

'He doesn't want you back, you know.' Maggie's thin lower lip curled. 'He may have agreed to bring you here, because his daddy asked him to. But it wasn't his idea.'

Joanna caught her breath. 'Thanks for the vote of confidence.'

'Don't get sassy with me, girl!'

'I'm not.' Joanna felt a little of her tension dissolve. Overt hostility she could deal with. It was the other kind that gnawed away at your composure. 'Don't worry, Maggie. I don't want your precious son.' She paused, and then a little imp of mischief made her add, softly, 'Not on a permanent basis, anyway.'

Cole's mother's face turned crimson. 'You—you——'

'*Ciao*,' murmured Joanna silkily, and, deciding to quit while she was ahead, she sauntered away.

CHAPTER SEVEN

JOANNA slept surprisingly well. She hadn't expected to. Not after the rather nerve-racking evening she had spent. But perhaps it was the fact that she hadn't slept much the night before. Whatever the reason, she lost consciousness as soon as her head touched the pillow, and it wasn't until one of the maids opened her curtains that she realised it was morning.

'Morning, miss—*ma'am*,' fumbled the girl, whom Joanna didn't recognise at all. Evidently she had been employed since Joanna left Tidewater, and her uncertain expression mirrored her inexperience.

'Miss will do,' said Joanna lazily, levering herself up on her pillows, as the delicious scent of coffee drifted to her nostrils. 'What's your name?'

'Rebecca, miss,' answered the girl, coming forward to lift the breakfast tray from the bedside cabinet. She set the legs at either side of Joanna's recumbent form, and fussed about, tidying the cutlery, which had slipped as she moved the tray.

'That's OK. Honestly.' Joanna held up a deterring hand. She looked down at the tray. 'Hmm. This looks wonderful.'

'Juice, eggs, and ham, toast and coffee,' declared Rebecca, blushing in confusion. 'Anything else I can get you, Miz Macallister?'

'It's Seton,' said Joanna drily. 'I'm Joanna Seton. I used to be Macallister, but not any more.'

'I understand.' Rebecca coloured again. 'You care for some pancakes, to go with your eggs?'

'Oh, no.' Joanna smiled, and shook her head. 'No, thanks. I doubt if I can manage all this.'

Rebecca hesitated. 'Well, if you're sure——'

'I'm sure,' declared Joanna, stifling a yawn. 'Um—what time is it?'

'Well,' Rebecca reflected, 'Miz Macallister said to bring up your tray at ten o'clock. I guess it must be a quarter after that now.'

'After *ten*!' Joanna was appalled. She never normally slept so late, and she could just imagine what Cole's mother would be thinking. Maggie had called her a lazy slut, in the not-too-distant past. And lying in bed till ten o'clock was as good as justifying the accusation.

But it wasn't true. It had never been true. If Joanna had stayed in bed in the past, it was because there had been nothing to get up for. Maggie wouldn't let her do anything; not a thing. And even her will to paint had been stifled in the closed atmosphere of Tidewater.

'Ain't nothing spoiling, miss,' Rebecca added, a little disturbed at Joanna's shocked reaction. 'Mr Macallister—he don't get up much before noon these days, and the boys—they're long gone.'

'The *boys*,' echoed Joanna ruefully, flopping back against her pillows, and Rebecca leapt forward to steady the tray.

'All 'cept Sandy,' she agreed, straightening up again. 'The young 'uns, they're all off to school. That Charley—she didn't wanna go. Said you and she had things to talk about. But Miz Macallister made her go, just the same.'

She would, thought Joanna broodingly, but she didn't say so. Besides, Charley's problems would have to wait. Right now, she was more concerned with finding out why Ryan Macallister had brought her here.

'I better go.' Rebecca seemed to think Joanna's silence was an indication that she had been gossiping too much, and it took quite an effort to assure her that this wasn't so.

'Thanks again,' Joanna offered, as the maid hurried towards the door. 'It's been nice meeting you. I hope we get to talk again.'

'Oh——' It was worth it to see Rebecca's cheeks bloom. 'Yes, I do, too,' she appended, and, with a little conspiratorial smile, she let herself out of the room.

After she was gone, Joanna wriggled up into a sitting position, and lifted the tray to one side of the huge, colonial four-poster. Then, sliding her feet to the floor, she stood up.

There was an expanse of cream shag carpet between where she was standing and the window, and she crossed it swiftly. The bedroom at her apartment in St John's Wood would have fitted a couple of times into this huge room. Apart from the bed, there were an assortment of heavy chests and cabinets, an antique *chaise-longue*, as well as the free-standing mirror Joanna had used the night before. There was also a walk-in closet, with fitted robes, a vanity unit and a long, velvet-padded bench to sit on.

Everything at Tidewater was larger than life, she thought wryly, drawing the louvred shutters aside and stepping out on to her balcony. Including its inhabitants, she conceded, with a certain tightening in her stomach.

It had been fairly warm in her bedroom, in spite of the shutters, but outside the heat was almost palpable already. It soon bathed her in a cloak of perspiration, and even the cotton nightshirt she was wearing clung damply to her skin. And this wasn't even the hottest it could get, she remembered, realising she would once have regarded this as only temperate. Yet, for all that, there was something decidedly sensual about such an abundance of nature's bounty, and the scents from the gardens below were positively intoxicating.

But it was the distant line of the ocean that caught her eyes. A breeze, both warm and salty, ruffled the loose tendrils that curled at her temple, and she put her hand against the back of her neck to lift the weight of hair away from her skin.

And that was when she saw Cole. He had evidently been out with the horses, and was presently unsaddling a huge blood bay in the paddock nearest to the house. He had seen her, too. As he straightened from loosening the girth, he looked straight at her balcony, and even from a distance she could sense his anger and his hostility.

But he looked good, she thought ruefully, her nerves prickling in unwilling anticipation. In tight jeans, leathers, and a shirt open halfway down his chest, he visibly breathed sexuality, and the heat that enveloped her at that moment had nothing to do with the climate. His hair, darkened by his exertions, lay damply against his head, and some uncontrollable part of her longed to run her fingers into the silvery gold strands clinging to his nape.

With oxygen suddenly becoming a scarce commodity, Joanna dragged a gulp of air into her lungs. Then, because she sensed his unwillingness to be caught looking at her balcony, she raised a hand in mocking acknowledgement. He might not want her here, but, whatever compulsion she possessed, he was not unaware of it. And, before he could do anything to rob her of that conviction, she turned and walked back into the room behind her.

Nevertheless, her own hands were not quite steady as she poured herself a cup of the coffee Rebecca had brought her. She perched on the edge of the bed to drink it, realising she wasn't used to this kind of sexual gamesmanship, and, while she was determined to keep the pressure on Cole, it was decidedly wearing on the nerves.

The eggs and ham were congealing on the plate, but she knew she couldn't face anything as substantial as a fried breakfast at this time. She was wondering if she could wrap them up in a paper napkin, and surreptitiously feed them to the dogs, when common sense reasserted itself. She didn't *have* to eat the meal, for heaven's sake. Just because, at one time, she would have done anything to avoid a confrontation with Cole's mother, she was allowing herself to be seduced by her surroundings. Now she could do exactly as she liked, and if Maggie had any comment to make about wasting food, so what?

Nevertheless, she knew she had to eat something. This was not the time to start starving herself. She would need all her wits about her in the next few hours, and a slice of toast and some orange juice sounded very palatable.

As it turned out, she couldn't resist eating two slices of toast spread with the chunky marmalade that was made from oranges grown on Tidewater land. Then, realising she was only delaying the inevitable, she went for her shower.

Half an hour later, she was ready to go downstairs. White shorts, and a scarlet vest, which emphasised the rounded curve of her breasts, seemed suitably provocative, and she had threaded her silky hair into a single plait that bobbed against her bare shoulder. She pushed her feet into rope-soled espadrilles, and then, with a final glance at the length of leg she was exposing, she threw herself a rueful grin, and picked up the tray.

Her suite of rooms was situated at the south-western corner of the house. A white-panelled corridor led to the galleried landing that overlooked the hall below, and she traversed it swiftly, pausing only once to absorb the once familiar configuration of the building. The rooms she and Cole used to occupy were in the opposite wing, and she guessed Maggie was responsible for her present situation. Or it might have been Cole, she conceded, guessing he probably occupied the other suite. The main apartments were all in the other half of the house, which was infinitely cooler than where Joanna was sleeping. Dear Maggie, she mused sardonically, starting down the stairs, always doing everything in her power to make her feel unwelcome.

The lower floor was cooler. It had been designed to allow for a free flow of air from front to back, and because the ceilings were high and wide it was possible to feel the benefit of the constantly turning fans. It reminded her that Cole had wanted to install an air-conditioning system, when she came to live at Tidewater. But his father had declared that what had been good enough for his father was good enough for him, and, in any case, it was an unnecessary expense.

Par for the course, she thought drily, glancing back up the stairs, and then did a double-take when she saw the subject of her musings gazing down at her from the upper floor.

'What you doing with that tray, girl?' Ryan Macallister demanded, and although his voice didn't carry the same authority it had once done, he startled her.

'The tray?' Joanna echoed, a little blankly. And then, quickly gathering her composure, 'I'm taking it to the kitchen.' She forced a polite smile. 'Ought you to be out of bed?'

Although Cole's father was clinging to the rails of the gallery with obvious necessity, his bony features took on an indignant scowl. 'I'm not dead yet,' he grated. 'Put that tray down, and get yourself up here. I want to talk to you.'

Joanna pressed her lips together, but she refused to be intimidated. 'After I've taken the tray to the kitchen,' she declared pleasantly. 'I won't be long——'

'Unless you want me to take a dive down these stairs, you'd better forget about the blasted tray and get your butt up here,' snapped Ryan harshly, and although Joanna wasn't totally convinced of his sincerity her conscience wouldn't let her take that risk.

With a helpless shrug of her shoulders, she deposited the tray on the iron-bound chest that stood in the lee of the stairs, and ran back up. She had guessed that Cole's father was hardly likely to ask her for help unless he had to, and certainly the fingers that grasped her arm for support felt suitably desperate.

'God-damned disease!' he muttered, causing her to stagger a little, as he transferred all his weight from the banister to her shoulder, and she realised he had not been joking about falling down the stairs. It really was an effort for him to get around at all.

'Take it easy,' she offered, as they made an unsteady progress back to his bedroom, and Ryan gave an obscene exclamation.

'Who're you to tell me to take it easy?' he exhorted breathlessly. 'Do you know what it's like to feel like a feeble-minded geriatric? Judas Priest, I'd be better off dead!'

'I don't think your family would agree with you,' murmured Joanna evenly, easing open his bedroom door with her hip, and helping him to cross the shagged carpet, and Ryan snorted.

'But you would, wouldn't you?' He took a laboured breath and heaved himself on to the side of the bed. 'You would, wouldn't you, girl? 'Cos you'd know I'd feel the same, if it was you.'

Joanna stepped back. He didn't need her help now. He was perfectly capable of ringing the bell beside the bed if he needed any further assistance. And, quite honestly, all she wanted to do was put as much distance between them as the limitations of Tidewater would allow.

But when she moved towards the door his voice stopped her. 'Where're you going?'

Joanna steeled herself and turned. 'I think you should rest, Mr Macallister.'

'Do you?' He made a sound of contempt. 'Just because I hurt your feelings, you're going to walk out on me, right?'

'Right.'

'Wrong.' He eased himself back against his pillows.
'We have to talk, and I don't know how much time I've
got.' He grimaced. 'Humour me.'

'Why should I?'

'Good question——' But he broke off to give a
hacking cough, and Joanna's resistance foundered.

'Look,' she said, 'I'll come back. I promise. When
you're feeling—stronger.'

'Huh.' He wiped his mouth on the back of his hand.
'I guess this is as strong as I'm going to get. Besides,
what do you care? Seeing me like this must be the
sweetest kind of revenge——'

'No!'

'No?'

'No.' Joanna swallowed. 'Hard as it may be for you
to believe, I do have some compassion.'

'Ah.' The old man's lips curled with evident satisfaction. 'I hoped you'd say that.'

'You did?' Joanna blinked. 'Why?'

'Because I want my son back,' declared Ryan
abruptly. 'And you're the only one who can do that for
me.'

'Your son?' Joanna felt totally confused. 'What son
are you talking about?'

'Don't play games with me, girl.' Her answer was
obviously not the one he had anticipated. 'You know
which son I mean. Cole, of course. I want you to tell
him I wasn't to blame for his brother's—accident!'

Joanna caught her breath. 'Nathan,' she said,
through dry lips. 'That's what all this is about:
Nathan!'

'*No!*' Ryan's voice was savage, and if he could have
reached her she was sure he would have slapped his
hand across her mouth to silence her. 'I've told you

what it's about,' he grated. 'Cole. I want Cole to treat
me like a father again. I want him to give me his respect. Dammit, the boy's my son! He owes me that
much.'

Joanna couldn't take this in. 'But I thought——'

'I don't care what you thought.' Ryan sucked in a
gurgling breath. 'Just listen to me.' The air whistled in
his lungs as he sought to calm himself. 'You did this.
You turned him away from me. You and your prissy
liberal ideas. Teaching people to want things they can't
have. I won't forgive you for what you did. I'll never
forgive you. But I need your help, dammit, and you're
going to give it to me!'

The air outside was doubly sweet after the cloying atmosphere of the sickroom. Stepping down from the
shaded columns of the veranda, Joanna crossed the
neatly cut turf to the paddock. Resting her hands on
the white-painted rail, she took several deep breaths of
the moist-scented air. Then, she sagged against the
fence. She felt drained, both emotionally and physically, and the elegant house behind her was a prison
from which she had made only a temporary escape. She
was trapped, and she knew it.

But of all the reasons why Ryan Macallister should
have wanted to see her, surely his request was the least
expected. To ask her to speak to Cole on his behalf! To
persuade Cole that his father had not been responsible
for what happened to Nathan; that he had played no
part in his death!

Joanna shivered in spite of the sun burning down on
her bare shoulders, and closed her eyes. When Cole
had told her his father wanted to see her, she hadn't
given it a lot of thought. She had been too intent on

making Cole's task as difficult as possible, and, as she had no intention of coming here, any curiosity she might have felt would have seemed a sign of weakness. Of course, when she had been so reckless as to change her mind, she had wondered then, but never in her wildest dreams could she have predicted Ryan's reasoning. Because she possessed an immutable core of compassion inside her, she had naturally assumed Cole's father must be the same. She had actually entertained the notion that he wanted to beg her forgiveness for what she had suffered at his and Maggie's hands.

She opened her eyes again, as a low moan escaped her lips. God! How wrong could you be? Ryan Macallister didn't have a compassionate muscle in his body. He was all unforgiving bone!

A lanky-legged colt, evidently used to being spoiled, came to nuzzle at her white-knuckled hands, and Joanna gave him a rueful smile.

'I'm afraid you're out of luck,' she said, displaying her empty palms. 'You and me both.'

'Feeling sorry for yourself?' enquired a drawling voice, and, turning her head, Joanna saw her ex-husband strolling across the grass towards her. For the past few moments, she had forgotten she had seen Cole in the paddock earlier, and now it took a distinct effort to face his undisguised hostility.

'I guess you'd like to think so,' she retorted, avoiding his gaze. She gestured towards the colt. 'What's his name?'

Cole halted at the other side of the fence, pulling an apple out of his pocket to give to the mare, who had come to see what her offspring was doing. 'He doesn't have a name yet,' he replied, his lean fingers easily breaking off a corner of the apple to give to the colt. 'Henry calls him Beau, for obvious reasons.'

'Hmm.' Joanna stretched out her hand and stroked the colt's dusky head. 'He is beautiful, isn't he?' And then, reacting to the name Cole had used, she looked up. 'Henry's still here?'

'Why wouldn't he be?' asked Cole shortly. 'He works here.'

'Yes, but——'

'Have you seen my father yet?'

Cole cut into her words with a taut enquiry, and although she would have preferred to pursue her line of thought, rather than his, the question was too urgent to be ignored.

'I—yes,' she said brittlely, deciding to be honest. 'That's why I'm here. I needed to get some fresh air.'

Cole's brows, which were several shades darker than his hair, descended in a glowering look. 'Must you always be so offensive?' he demanded, putting his hand on the top bar, and vaulting over the railing. 'The man's dying, for God's sake. Can't you show him some respect?'

'As you do?'

The words sprang, unguardedly, from her tongue, and she was hardly surprised when Cole reacted to them. 'What the hell do you mean?' he muttered, glaring at her with angry eyes, and Joanna's heart skipped a beat as he thrust his face close to hers.

'Why, what do you think I mean, darlin'?' she taunted, realising this was her only means of defence. She lifted her hand and let her knuckles slide down his cheek, which was roughened by a fine stubbling of silvery-blond beard. 'I was only teasing, wasn't I? Everyone knows, you're Daddy's blue-eyed boy!'

Cole's hand clamped about her wrist, dragging it down to his side. 'You can't wait to cause trouble, can you?' he snarled, and although his grasp was painful the burning frustration in his eyes wasn't.

'Careful, darlin',' she murmured, her slim fingers reaching out to stroke the taut muscle of his thigh, exposed by the tight-fitting denim. 'Your mother might be watching, and we wouldn't want her to think we can't get along.'

CHAPTER EIGHT

JOANNA ate lunch with Maggie and Ben. Cole didn't come to the table, and Ben told her that Joe and Alicia had built their own house on the property, and spent most of their time there. The three younger members of the family were at school, of course, and the conversation during the meal was decidedly strained. But at least Ryan Macallister didn't join them, for which she was grateful. She needed time to decide what she was going to do, before confronting him again.

After lunch, she learned that Cole had gone into Beaumaris. Maggie took great delight in informing her that he wouldn't be back until that evening. Joanna managed not to show any emotion to his mother, but she was annoyed just the same. If she'd known he was leaving, she'd have found some way to get him to take her with him. But probably he had known that, too, she acknowledged, which was why he hadn't mentioned it.

So, unwilling to risk another encounter with Ryan Macallister, Joanna spent the afternoon in her room. It did cross her mind that she could go down to the stables, and renew her acquaintance with Henry, but she was loath to open that particular can of worms today. Instead, she kicked off her espadrilles, and stretched out on the bed. Perhaps she'd feel better after a nap.

But she didn't go to sleep. Her brain was too active to allow her to relax. Even though the events of the morning had taken their toll, her mind kept re-running the reasons that had brought her here. She'd thought she'd put the past behind her. She'd thought she was immune to anything the Macallisters could to to her. But coming back to Tidewater, meeting Cole's family again, had acted like a catalyst on her emotions. She might be tougher than she used to be, but she wasn't out of danger.

How strange it was, she thought, that one small incident could change your whole life. She certainly hadn't expected a faulty fuel pump to be her stepping-stone to fame and fortune. And yet that was exactly how it had happened.

As the youngest child of older parents, born when the offspring closest to her in age was already ten years old, Joanna had lived a fairly solitary existence until she went to school. She had become used to entertaining herself, and her aptitude for drawing did not go unnoticed. But, although her parents were proud of her artistic skills, they did not consider them a viable occupation. Joanna was encouraged to work hard at her academic studies, and even though she insisted on leaving school at eighteen, to give her more time to study her art, she spent her days in the merchant bank, which her father's family had founded.

When the tutor at the night class she attended suggested putting a couple of her paintings on exhibition at the local library, Joanna had never expected anyone to be interested. But Grace, who had been driving back from an exhibition in Sussex, developed a fault with her car in Guildford High Street, and while it was being mended she wandered into the little gallery.

Of course, Joanna's success didn't happen overnight. But Grace had sufficient faith in her to offer her the chance to show her work in the West End gallery she managed. Just one painting, at first, and, when that sold fairly quickly, another, until by the time Joanna was twenty-one she was able to give up the bank, and devote herself to her art.

In the meantime, she and Grace had become close friends. In spite of the difference in their ages, they had a lot in common, and after Joanna found herself a flat in London Grace became her agent as well. And, naturally, they shared confidences. Grace heard all about Joanna's lonely childhood, and Joanna learned that Grace had once been married to an American, and that she had two teenage sons living in South Carolina.

Which was why, when the tall American strolled into the gallery one day, when Joanna was alone, and asked where Grace was, she gave him a rather cool reception. She had guessed he must be some relation of Grace's ex-husband—in spite of her antipathy towards him, she had not been able to deny the attraction of his lazy southern voice—but, as he was too old to be either of Grace's sons, she had assumed Grace wouldn't be too pleased to see him.

However, as with so many things about Cole, she thought ruefully, she had been wrong. When Grace returned, fortunately only a few minutes later, she had greeted him with real affection, and it had been obvious that, whatever relationship she had with her ex-husband, his nephew was a great favourite of hers.

And, because Grace had been so insistent that they should become friends, Joanna had unwillingly accepted the invitation to join them for dinner that evening. Ray Marsden had joined them, too. To make up a foursome, Grace had said, although subsequent events had led Joanna to make a different interpretation of that arrangement. In any event, they had all enjoyed one of Grace's home-cooked meals, served in the tiny apartment she occupied above the gallery. And afterwards Cole had taken her home.

Looking back now, Joanna recognised that, despite her initial misgivings about him, she had probably fallen in love with Cole that very evening. He had been so attractive, so amusing—and so downright sexy— that she hadn't stood a chance. Although he was only four years older than she, he was aeons older in experience, and while common sense warned her to be careful her leaping senses had left her little room for compromise.

Naturally, he had known better than to rush her. There had been no furtive grapplings in the hall outside her apartment, no abortive attempts to invade her space without her involvement. That first evening, he had escorted her home without even attempting to kiss her goodnight. He had been polite, and courteous, and she had been the one left with a disturbing sense of loss. Indeed, she had half wondered if she had only imagined the lingering looks he had cast in her direction during the course of the evening. Perhaps he wasn't attracted to her, after all. Perhaps it had just been good old-fashioned southern gallantry.

There had been no reason for her to go to the gallery the following day, but, after spending a wasted morning at her easel, she decided to go for a walk. It was early summer, and the rhododendrons were out in the park. A good enough reason, she thought, for her to cast a critical eye over them.

She stayed out for a couple of hours. She was loath to go back to face a blank sheet of sketching paper. She knew exactly where she wanted to be, but she wasn't confident enough to go for it. Instead, she bought French bread and cream cakes. She'd decided to console herself with starch.

But when she got back to her apartment she found she had a visitor. Cole was sitting on the low wall that skirted the garden of the Victorian conversion. In tight-fitting jeans that clung to his long legs, and a black T-shirt, he looked lean, and tanned, and muscular, his brown hands resting on the wall at either side of his lazy, lounging frame.

The colour raced to Joanna's face, but she couldn't help it. She had been thinking about him all day, and every image she'd had had been accurate. He was just as attractive as she remembered, and her artist's eye lingered lovingly on his broad shoulders and rippling muscles. The belt that secured his jeans rested low on his narrow hips, the silver buckle drawing her eyes like a magnet. Seduced them, too, to the worn cloth of his fly, and the sun-bleached denim that cupped his sex.

But she knew, if she was honest, it was not his male beauty, as a subject for her easel, that caused the blood to race madly through her veins at that moment. For the first time in her life, she knew what it was like to actually *want* a man. She wanted to look at him, and touch him, and for him to touch her. But she hadn't the faintest notion of how to bring that about.

In an age when behaving promiscuously was the rule rather than the exception, Joanna was still a virgin. Oh, she had had boyfriends. She was young and, in her eyes, moderately attractive, and she had never had any lack of admirers. But, perhaps as a result of being born to older parents, she had acquired their values, rather than those of her own generation. In consequence, she had always regarded sex as a fairly overrated occupation. Certainly, none of the young men she had dated had inspired any great desire to experiment in that way. Which was why her instantaneous attraction to Cole was so astonishing to her. Astonishing, and disturbing. She wasn't entirely sure she wanted that kind of complication in her life.

'Hi,' he said, getting up at her approach, and taking the bag of groceries from her. 'Let me help you with that.'

Joanna's tongue made a hasty circuit of her upper lip. 'Have—have you been waiting long?' she asked—as if she'd been expecting him, she chided herself irritably. 'Um—I've been shopping.'

The banality of her response made her cringe, but she couldn't help it. She didn't know what else to say. If only she had put on a dress before she went out, she fretted. Her purple dungarees were splashed with paint.

'I guess I should have called first.' Cole removed any sense of embarrassment with his easy charm. 'But I didn't know your last name, and I didn't care to ask Aunt Grace.' He gave a rueful grin. 'She might not have approved of my seeing you again.'

Joanna blinked. 'Oh?' She lifted her slim shoulders, and the shoulder-strap of her dungarees fell off one shoulder. 'Why not?'

Cole's mouth flattened. 'She might think I wasn't to be trusted,' he conceded softly, putting out his hand and restoring the strap to its proper position. His fingers lingered against her shoulder and, although she was wearing a cotton shirt under the dungarees, his touch seared her flesh. 'She's very fond of you.'

'And—and I'm very fond of her,' stammered Joanna, shifting so that his hand fell harmlessly away. 'She—she's been very good to me.'

'The way I see it, you've been pretty good to her, too,' responded Cole. 'Without the commission she's taken from your work, she wouldn't have been able to buy into the gallery. Marsden's no fool. He saw the advantages of tying Grace into that partnership.'

Joanna moved her head. 'I'm sure you're exaggerating.'

'I don't think so.' Cole regarded her steadily for a few disturbing moments, and then glanced behind him. 'Are you going to invite me in?'

'What? Oh!' Joanna realised she was being unforgivably rude. Whatever she felt about him, he had taken the trouble to come here, and he had been holding her shopping bag for the past few minutes. 'I—of course.' She fumbled for her keys. 'It's up several flights of stairs, I'm afraid.'

'Tell me about it.' Cole was sardonic. 'You folks don't go much for elevators, do you?'

Joanna unlocked the outer door, and smiled. 'The gallery?' she suggested, and Cole nodded.

'You got it,' he agreed. 'No wonder Grace keeps her figure. I'd be a physical wreck if I had to climb those stairs every day.'

Joanna led the way up the first flight of stairs. 'I doubt it,' she murmured, giving him a surreptitious glance, and Cole's eyes narrowed appraisingly.

'Do you?' He shifted the shopping bag to his other arm. 'But you don't know anything about me—yet.'

'I—I don't think you're likely to be—to be worn out by a few stairs,' she insisted, as they started up the second flight.

'Is that so?' Cole's tone of enquiry brought her eyes to him again, and she missed a step, and had to grab for the banister.

'Y-yes,' she answered, feeling a complete fool. And thereafter she concentrated on what she was doing until they reached her floor.

Joanna's apartment was on the third floor of the old building. Originally used as the servants' quarters, in the days when the house had been lived in by only one family, the rooms had been small and airless, with tiny windows set up high in the walls. But a far-sighted developer had knocked down walls, heightened ceilings, and installed wide picture windows that gave a magnificent view of the surrounding area. He had also had the foresight to enlarge an existing skylight, and nowadays that room was used as Joanna's studio.

Now, Joanna unlocked the door, and led Cole into a rather untidy living-room. When she was working, she tended not to notice her surroundings, but now, looking at the room through his eyes, she wished she had concentrated on her housework, instead of mooching about in the park.

It was basically a two-bedroomed apartment, with the kitchen adjoining the living-room, and her bedroom, bathroom, and the studio opening from the hall that led off the living-room. There was no dining-room, as such, and she was sure it was much smaller than any apartment Cole was used to—except perhaps Grace's. But it hadn't been cheap, and she was proud of it. It was a symbol of her success, and as such she loved the independence it signified.

While she was fretting over the wilted carnations, drooping in their vase, and the papers strewn across the couch, Cole had leaned against the door to close it, and walked across the room to admire the view.

'Impressive,' he said, both arms wrapped around the supermarket bag, and, remembering her manners, Joanna went to take it from him. 'Just show me where you want it,' he intoned huskily, and, aware of the *double entendre*, she turned jerkily towards the kitchen.

'Here,' she said, gesturing towards the least cluttered work-top, and Cole deposited the bag where she had indicated. But, when he gave the kitchen an equally interested inspection, she added, hurriedly, 'I'm sorry the place is such a mess. I—er—I wasn't expecting visitors.'

Cole's eyes danced. 'You only clean the place when you're expecting company, is that right?'

Joanna flushed. 'No,' she said defensively. 'It's not usually like this.'

'No sweat.' Cole shrugged his broad shoulders, and tucked his thumbs into the low belt that circled his hips. 'I didn't come to see the apartment anyway.'

Joanna stiffened a spine that weakened every time he looked at her in quite that way. 'If—if you'd like to go and sit down, I'll make some coffee,' she declared, in her most repressive tone, but Cole made no move to do as she had requested.

'How about we get a beer, and sit down together?' he suggested, and Joanna's stomach hollowed alarmingly.

'I'm afraid I—don't have any beer,' she offered apologetically. 'Just—just Coke.'

'Coke's fine,' Cole assured her, nodding towards the fridge-freezer. 'In there?'

Joanna nodded, watching helplessly as he swung open the fridge door, and took two cans of Coke from the shelf. Illuminated by the light inside, his face was disturbingly sensual, and she wondered at her own ability to handle the situation. But when the door closed, and the light went out, her mother's training asserted itself again. 'The—er—the glasses are in here,' she murmured, opening one of the wall cupboards.

But Cole only gave her a lazy glance. 'Tastes better out of a can,' he assured her. Handing her one of the ice-cold containers, he tore the tab off his and raised the can to his lips. The brown column of his throat rippled as he swallowed the liquid, and Joanna couldn't help watching him, her eyes as wide and startled as those of a mesmerised rabbit.

Then, gathering her scattered senses, she dragged her gaze away. For heaven's sake, she chided herself, he was only a man! But it was hard to concentrate on anything and her attention slipped again, so that the tab came off unevenly, and snagged the pad of her thumb.

Cole had started to walk into the living-room, with the can still raised to his lips, when he heard her muffled exclamation. Glancing round, he saw at once what had happened, and, slamming down his drink, he came to take her hand.

'How the hell did you do that?' he exclaimed, but his tone was indulgent. Taking the injured finger into his mouth, he licked the blood away. 'What a pity it wasn't your lip. Then I'd have had an excuse to do this.' And, lowering his head, he brushed her mouth with his tongue.

Joanna's legs wobbled. He was fast, she thought, trying to keep a hold on her senses. He hadn't been in the apartment fifteen minutes, and already he had kissed her. Or was that really kissing? It hadn't happened to her before, so she didn't really know.

'You OK?' he asked, and she realised he was watching her fairly closely. Close enough to glimpse the uncertainty in her eyes, she thought. Close enough to realise she was getting out of her depth.

'I'm—fine,' she got out hurriedly, her tone tense and clipped. 'I think I'd better get a plaster. I don't want to get blood everywhere.'

'A plaster?' Cole looked puzzled for a moment, and then his face cleared. 'Oh, you mean a Band-aid.' He nodded. 'Right.'

'Right.' Joanna drew her hand firmly away, breathing a sigh of relief, when he let her. 'Why—er—why don't you go and finish your drink? I won't be a minute.'

Cole didn't move. 'Is something wrong?' he queried, and Joanna, who had started rummaging about in a drawer for the packet of Elastoplast she knew was there somewhere, gave him a guilty look.

'Something wrong?' she echoed, trying to sound surprised. 'No. No. Why would there be?'

'You tell me.'

Joanna shook her head, feeling more and more awkward. 'I don't know what you mean.' She found the box of plasters, and her fingers fastened weakly about it. 'Really—I won't be long.'

Cole regarded her intently for what seemed an inordinate amount of time, and then, moving forward, he took the box from her. 'Let me do it,' he said, and although Joanna wanted to argue it was easier to give in.

Besides, she had to admit later, he had made a neat job of wrapping the plaster round her thumb. It was certainly neater than she could have managed. But, when she opened her mouth to thank him, he fore-stalled her.

'Tell me something,' he said, holding on to her fingers when she would have withdrawn them again. 'Did I get the wrong signal here?'

Joanna swallowed. 'The wrong signal?'

'Yeah.' Cole smoothed his thumb over the back of her hand. 'Do you want me to go?'

Joanna's jaw sagged, and she moved her shoulders in a helpless gesture. Her skin was prickling with awareness and, somewhere down in her stomach, she could feel a dull pain. 'I—why, no,' she said at last. 'Why should you think that?'

Cole shrugged. 'The way you acted when I touched you,' he replied.

Joanna tried to act casually. 'You're touching me now,' she pointed out lightly, but Cole didn't smile.

'You know what I mean,' he said flatly. 'Is this a turn-off?'

Such words he used! Joanna shook her head. She didn't know how to answer him. She had never met anybody who asked such personal questions before. Her dealings with his sex had been fairly simple up till now. The men she had dated had been the kind of men who let her dictate the pace of their relationships. And, because she had never been emotionally involved before, their encounters had never been in any danger of getting out of hand. But Cole was different. She had known that as soon as she met him. What she hadn't recognised was *how* different. And, in her eagerness to know him better, she had walked into a situation she simply didn't know how to deal with.

'I don't think—we should rush things,' she got out at last, wondering how the abrasive brush of his thumb could cause such havoc inside her. 'We—we hardly know one another.'

'Don't we?' With a little jerk, he brought her unwary body towards him. Then, before she had a chance to protest, he released her fingers and put both his hands on her hips. The weight of those hard hands burned through the thin material of her dungarees, and because, underneath, her hips were bare, they were disturbingly intimate, too. 'So,' he crooned softly, 'let's get to know one another better.'

'Oh, really!' Joanna's hands spread against his shirt-front. It was a puny defence and she knew it, but events were moving far too swiftly. 'I wish you wouldn't do this.'

'Do what?' asked Cole huskily, looking down into the open V of her shirt, and causing a wave of heat to envelop her. 'Say, are you wearing anything under this coverall?'

'You know I am.' Joanna's response wasn't hesitant this time, and Cole's eyes glimmered with undisguised amusement. But, conversely, his humour upset her almost as much as his advances had done, and in a tight, angry tone she added, 'I suppose you think this is very funny!'

Cole's eyes softened. 'Don't be so touchy.' He lifted one hand and stroked it down her cheek. 'Is all your skin as soft as this?'

Joanna's breathing felt constricted. 'Cole——'

'Hmm.' His hand had left her cheek, and had now coiled around her neck. His thumb was rubbing the skin on the underside of her jaw, as if he was testing for an answer to the question he had asked earlier, and his

fingers beneath her hair were hard against her nape. It
was strange, she thought bemusedly, how his hands
were so hard, while hers were so soft. Everything about
him was hard and masculine, and she had the craziest
urge to lean into him and feel his hardness right down
her body...

'Cole, I think—I think we should go into the other
room,' she stammered, as the realisation of what was
happening to her brought her briefly to her senses. 'I—
I could make us something to eat——'

'I've got something to eat,' retorted Cole huskily,
bending his head to stroke his tongue from a point just
below her ear to the curve of shoulder he was exposing. He tipped off the strap of her dungarees, and
slipped his hand into the neckline of her shirt. 'God,
you taste good,' he muttered, taking a tender circle of
flesh between his teeth and tugging it into his mouth.
'So good...'

Joanna trembled. All the juices in her body seemed
to be melting and expanding, rising to the surface of
her skin and dissolving her resistance. She knew she
was going to have a bruise on her neck later, but there
was nothing she could do about it. Her senses were
blinding her to everything but the needs he was building inside her, and her eyes closed instinctively, shut-
ting out the world.

He pulled her against him, his hand finding the
swollen fullness of her breast. The engorged areola
surged against his palm, and he rubbed its sensitive tip
urgently. Then he lowered his head and dragged the
aching nipple into his mouth.

Joanna's legs sagged. Like a drowning woman now,
she wrapped her arms around him, and pressed her
face against his chest. His shirt was half open, and the

hair that clustered in the V was rough against her cheek. But the scent of his skin was heavenly, and she opened her mouth wide to taste his fragrance.

Cole moved into her then, imprisoning her against the wall behind her, and jerking her mouth up to his. His hungry tongue surged into her mouth, fierce and possessive, and his jeans-clad thigh was insistent as it eased its way between her legs. His assault was demanding, but sweetly sensual. And nothing had prepared Joanna for her own need to respond.

This couldn't be happening, she told herself in one lucid moment, when the coolness of the air around her thighs warned her that her dungarees were in a heap around her ankles. Cole had flipped the other strap from her shoulder, and the loose-fitting overalls had slipped cleanly down her body. Now his hands were cupping her rounded bottom as he tugged her even closer, and not even the tight-fitting denim could hide his huge arousal.

But what troubled her most was her own willingness to give in to him. The firm pressure of his mouth and the sensuous invasion of his tongue were becoming as important to her as breathing. Innocent she might be, ignorant even, of the many forms of sexuality. But her instincts were all rebellious, and her blood felt as if it was on fire. The touch of his hands against her bare flesh; the musky scent of his body. She could think of nothing more desirable than to feel his naked flesh against hers. And, acting without thinking, she tentatively touched the bulge of his erection.

'Oh, *God*!'

Cole's reaction was—not entirely unexpectedly—violent. When her slim artist's fingers strayed along the straining teeth of his zip, he visibly shuddered. With a burning impatience, he sloughed off his belt and tore open his jeans. Then, he took her down on to the floor in the same instant that his hard manhood surged into her hands.

'God, you're beautiful!' he muttered, cradling her head on one arm, and using the other to peel away her shirt. And, although common sense was telling her she must not let this go any further, the admiration in his eyes was an overpowering temptation.

Besides, her curiosity about him was just as compelling. Probably more so, she admitted, looking down at his magnificent body. It was the first time she had seen a man naked and aroused, and even though he had only bared his sex its rampant power was mesmerising.

Cole's head blocked her view, as he bent to lay a trail of kisses from the tip of one breast to the hollow of her navel. His forefinger hooked into the band of her bikini briefs, tugging them out of his way, and then his mouth concluded its journey in the moist curls that hid her womanhood.

She jerked then, her inexperienced limbs responding to the fever he was creating. Her legs splayed, and then she clamped them tight together. Dear God, she thought disbelievingly, did she want him to think she was cheap? But, in spite of all her misgivings, Cole eased her legs apart again. While his tongue searched the helpless cavern of her mouth, his finger slid inside her, finding the dew-drenched honeycomb, and the sensitive bud of her sex.

Her eyes, which had drifted shut, now opened in alarm, but Cole's expression was sensuous, revealing he was just as involved as she was. And she relaxed as she looked at him, revelling in the knowledge that he found her beautiful. He was beautiful, too; beautiful and sexy. She wanted him to go on touching her, and she shuddered at the needs he was arousing.

'Do it,' he said huskily, and she realised he could read her thoughts as well. 'Here.' He took one of her trembling hands and laid it on him. 'Yes, that's right. You're a natural. Oh, God, Jo, I want you. And I don't think I can wait any longer.'

CHAPTER NINE

'GOD, JO, you should have told me!'

Cole lay beside her on the cool tiles of the kitchen floor, one arm raised across his eyes, and the other lying by his side. It was funny, Joanna thought, but she could never have imagined she would lose her virginity in such unlikely surroundings. When she had occasionally daydreamed about how it would happen, a bed had always been involved. A bed; and champagne; and a rather fetching négligé.

'It doesn't matter,' she said now, wondering if he regretted it already. For herself, she hardly knew what she was feeling. It had been so much less—and yet so much more—than she had anticipated that she felt almost numb. She was shocked by what had happened, yes; but she was also anxious that it might never happen again.

And she wanted it to happen again, she knew that. Whatever kind of a disappointment it had been for Cole, she had experienced feelings she had not even dreamed were possible. He had invaded the limits of her sexuality, and time and place meant nothing, compared to the sensations that had gripped her.

Even now, she remembered every moment of his possession. The surging heat of his manhood, pressing its way inside her. The momentary withdrawal, when he had felt her inexperience. He had wanted to draw back then, she knew it. But her hands clutching his buttocks, and the undoubted invitation of her expanding muscles, had compelled him to go on. Besides, there was a limit to his endurance, she had guessed that for herself. He had wanted her. He had said so. And the aching fullness of his loins had demanded its own release.

But he had drawn back before his shuddering spasms informed her of his climax. And the mindless race inside her had come abruptly to its end. But, even though the little knowledge she possessed told her that there had to be more, she was inordinately grateful that it had been Cole who had taken her virginity. No other man had ever aroused the feelings inside her that he aroused, and, although she knew she ought to feel some measure of regret for what had happened, she didn't.

And, when he rolled on to his elbow to look down at her with rueful eyes, she felt no embarrassment for her nudity. On the contrary, if nothing else, Cole had taught her that she was beautiful, in his eyes at least, and she moved instinctively, unconsciously inviting his approval.

'It matters,' he said at last, but there was a sensual twist to his mouth as he bent to touch her lips with his. 'God, Jo, I've never done anything like this before.'

'Have you wanted to?' she asked, unknowingly provocative, and he shook his head, the sweat-streaked blond hair brushing her sensitised skin.

'No,' he admitted gruffly, but when her arm curved around his neck he couldn't prevent the kiss from deepening.

This time, Joanna's tongue was the invader, teasing his lips and his tongue, until Cole lost control and

drove down deep into her mouth. Joanna was overwhelmed with the need to get closer to him. Half ex-
perimentally, she coiled one leg about him, revelling in
the way it brought the lower half of his body nearer to
hers. Suddenly, she could feel the rigid thrust of his
hips, and the hairy tautness of his thigh riding against
hers. But it was the muscles between his legs that
strained against her. He was already hard again, she
discovered. Hard and hot, and as satin-smooth as vel-
vet against her stomach.

'We shouldn't do this,' he muttered, when her hand
stroked possessively over his buttocks, and Joanna
found the courage to look up at him.

'Why not?' she breathed. 'Don't you want to?' But
her question became unimportant when he crushed her
beneath him again. For Cole wasn't immune to the
needs of his own body, and the readiness of hers was an
irresistible temptation. She was wet with longings he
had created, and her tight, resistant muscles closed eagerly about him.

Fever gripped Joanna's body. She was still aroused
from their previous coupling, and the emotions she had
felt before sprang into fervent life. Like an athlete who
had faltered before the final hurdle, her body was eager to redress the balance, and when Cole's rhythm
quickened she matched him pace for pace.

And, in so doing, she found her own senses slipping
away. A mindless pleasure was encompassing her
limbs, melting her bones, drowning her inhibitions. She
wasn't aware of making any sound at all, yet she could
hear gasps, and moans, and anguished pleas escaping
her lips.

'Say it's good,' Cole breathed against her temple,
and the voice that answered him sounded nothing like

her own. It was soft, and husky, and incredibly sensual, and Cole's satisfaction took him even deeper inside her.

'Yes, yes,' she cried, her nails digging into his shoulders, and the wild excitement that had been building and expanding inside her became unbearably sweet. And then it happened. A pulsing wave of pure pleasure enveloped her, sweeping her up and up, until she was half afraid she was going to lose consciousness, and she didn't want that. She didn't want to lose a moment of such incredible beauty, and when Cole would have drawn back she wrapped her legs around him. The flooding heat as he spilled himself inside her just added to her enjoyment, and this time when his body shook she held him close to her breast.

Of course, afterwards, after Cole had gone, and she was alone, Joanna was appalled at the wanton way she had acted. That she, who had always regarded herself as being totally self-possessed, should have lost control so completely was bad enough. But that she should have done so with a man she had known less than twenty-four hours seemed almost indecent. He would think she had been desperate to lose her virginity, she thought, and for days after that she refused to answer either the telephone or the doorbell, in case it shouldn't be him. She had convinced herself he wouldn't want to contact her again, and she submerged herself in her work to the exclusion of everything else.

Eventually, it was Grace who smoked her out; Grace who informed her that, far from not wanting to see her again, Cole had been practically going out of his head with worry, because he couldn't reach her. And, because he was sure Joanna must blame him for what had happened, he had confided in his aunt, and asked for her assistance.

Later, Joanna had understood what it must have cost him to approach Grace. When she learned more about him, and about his background, she had realised how galling it must have been for Ryan Macallister's son to ask a woman for anything, particularly someone his father both disliked and despised.

But, at the time, she had been too overwhelmed by Cole's interest in her to consider how his family might react to another Englishwoman in their midst. She and Cole had seen one another every day, and their relationship just got better and better. So much so that Cole delayed his return to South Carolina long enough to persuade her to marry him.

Of course, Grace had had misgivings, and she had voiced them. The Macallisters were a very close family, she said. They weren't like Joanna's parents, who had taken to Cole from the start. On top of which, Tidewater was another world, with its own laws, and its own traditions. She hadn't been happy there, and she didn't know if Joanna would be, particularly as Cole was just as possessive as his uncle.

But Joanna hadn't wanted to listen, even though the only arguments she and Cole had were about her work. He resented the time she devoted to it and not to him, and, although she was convinced that once they were married it wouldn't be a problem, it was a complication she had foolishly ignored.

The wedding was planned for the end of June, and Cole had flown home to give his family the news. But when he had flown back again, only a couple of days before the wedding, not one of his family had come with him. 'They couldn't leave the plantation,' he had said, his face reddening. His younger brother and sisters were still in school, and there was simply too much to do, particularly since he was away, too.

And Joanna, not wanting to embarrass him any further, had accepted his excuses. But Grace had had no such reservations. The night before the wedding, she had warned Joanna of what she might have to face at Tidewater, and if she hadn't been fathoms deep in love Joanna might have listened to her. As it was, she convinced herself that Grace was exaggerating, and the weeks immediately following their wedding were the happiest weeks she could remember.

But that had been while they were on honeymoon, she conceded drily. Cole had taken her to Tahiti, and during those exotic days and nights she had had no doubts that nothing and no one could come between them. They had been timeless days, when they had been drunk with each other's possession. Days of sun and happiness, and luscious, languid nights. Then they had returned to Tidewater.

To begin with, Joanna managed to convince herself that they would work it out. Even though his mother made no secret of her disapproval of the marriage, and his father was barely civil, she refused to lose heart. When they left the plantation house, and got a home of their own, she told herself, his parents' attitude wouldn't matter. In the meanwhile, it was up to her to try and make it friendly.

And, although Cole's parents could control his days, she controlled his nights. While the heat and the humidity of midsummer made other people terse and irritable, she and Cole continued to revel in those hot, sleepless nights. He taught her so much about her body, and she was a willing pupil. She learned that even the most unlikely areas could prove wildly erotic, and Cole spent hours tracing nerves and sensitive pulses, and setting them on fire with his tongue. Their love-making just got better and better, and she responded to his demands with all the urgency of her youth.

But, ironically enough, it was that very eagerness to prove herself that sowed the seeds of her destruction. In trying to avoid conflict, Joanna only joined the family for meals if Cole was going to be there. She had found her skin was too thin to withstand the barbs and insults his father threw around when he wasn't, and she was too proud to tell Cole what they were doing to her.

Besides, what could she have said? Cole himself admitted she wasn't used to the kind of life they led at Tidewater, and he would be the first to agree that she was much softer than the southern women he was used to. And to complain that his mother regarded any efforts she made to help around the house with contempt would hardly arouse his indignation. He would probably have wondered why she cared, without understanding how important it was for Joanna to find her own space.

Even their own rooms were not sacrosanct. Maggie thought nothing of coming into their bedroom without knocking, except when she knew her son was there. Flowers were rearranged; furniture Joanna had altered was replaced; and even her closet was not free from his mothers' influence. Favourite dresses went missing; shirts she especially liked developed unexplained tears, or lost buttons; and any time she wore anything at all provocative, she was made to feel so cheap that she started buying clothes that didn't show her shape.

Just thinking about it now made Joanna feel physically sick. Gradually, over a period of time, they had caused her to doubt herself, and her own sanity, and once that happened she was on a downward spiral.

But that had come later—after the illness, which had caused the first faint cracks to appear in their relationship. Because of the heat, and because she was neither eating nor sleeping enough, those long passionate nights took their toll. A chill developed quickly into pneumonia, and while she was weak and helpless Cole's parents took their chance.

By the time she was lucid enough to know what was happening, Cole's belongings had been moved into another suite of rooms entirely. His mother had only been thinking of her, he said, when Joanna grew strong enough to offer her objections. There was no way he could have continued to share her room without disturbing her. And they all wanted to do their best, so that she would soon be well again.

It was a reasonable excuse, and one with which Cole evidently agreed, but Joanna was uneasy. She was more uneasy still, when Ryan Macallister set up a business trip for Cole to South America, thus delaying his return to her bed even longer. In other circumstances, Cole assured her, she could have gone with him. But as she had been so ill...

The night before he went away, she had tried to talk to him about their future. When were they going to get a home of their own? she pleaded. They'd been married more than three months now, and it was time she started looking after her husband herself.

Cole had avoided a direct answer, she remembered. Now was not the time for her to start worrying about things like that, he said. She needed to get her strength

back. Better she leave the housekeeping to his mother
for the time being. If he remembered correctly, do-
mestic duties had never been her strong point.

He was away a month, and, although she spoke to
him frequently on the telephone, by the time he came
back, things had changed. Joanna supposed she had
been partly responsible for that change, but how could
she have known what her innocent befriending of
Nathan Smith would stir up? At the time, she had just
been desperate for some stimulating adult conversation.

She sighed. Perhaps she had been naïve, she pon-
dered. It wasn't as if all the Macallisters had been hos-
tile. Ben and Joe had been quite friendly, so long as
their father wasn't around; and the twins, especially
Charley, had developed quite a crush on their new sister-in-law. And there was Sandy—though he had been
too young to really count.

But, perhaps because she was becoming so sensitive
to any criticism levelled at her, Joanna never felt entirely relaxed around the house. She had done very little sketching or painting since she left England, so now,
once again, she endeavoured to submerge her unhap-
piness in her work. There was certainly plenty of scope
for an artist among the vivid varieties of trees and
shrubs about the plantation, and she took to taking her
sketch book with her every time she went for a walk.

Although she never ventured too far from the house,
she became familiar with the stables, and the paddocks, and the salt marshes beyond. She often curled
up beside the river, lulled by the gentle music of the
water, or scrambled over the mud-flats at low tide, in
search of shells. Although her olive skin never tanned,

it grew sun-warmed and healthy, and her hair grew long and wind-tossed, accentuating her gypsy appearance.

And, during this time, it never occurred to her not to be familiar with the workers on the plantation. The grooms around the stables, the hands who exercised the horses, even the maids in the house, all benefited from her friendly disposition. She didn't think it had been a conscious effort to oppose Cole's father and mother. It was just her way. But she never, ever dreamed where her attitude might lead her.

Nathan didn't work on the plantation. Although she didn't know that the morning she surprised him on the river-bank. He had been leaning out over the river, trailing his hand in the water, and at that time it was doubtful which of them had been the most shocked by the encounter.

But when he jumped to his feet, with the evident intention of leaving, Joanna had stopped him. 'What were you doing?' she asked, tucking her sketch pad under her arm, and stepping across the grassy bank towards him. She looked down into the water, but could see nothing of value. 'Did you drop something?'

Nathan shook his head. He was a handsome young man, with dark curly hair, brown skin, and the broad nose and full mouth that spoke of a mixed heritage. Joanna assumed he lived in the shacks that bordered the estate to the west. Many of the workers lived in the shacks at Palmer's Point, and Cole had said that he and his father were planning on re-housing the families. However, after listening to Ryan Macallister's views on his poorer employees, and learning of his contempt for people who had more children than they could afford, Joanna was less convinced. She had the feeling that, whatever Cole said, his father was not as committed as his son.

'So what were you doing?' she asked now, and although the young man would have obviously preferred to avoid answering he stood his ground.

'Tickling fish,' he said, his lean features taking on a rueful expression. 'I wasn't taking many. Only one or two.'

Joanna shook her head. 'You mean—you can actually catch fish that way?' she exclaimed. Then she saw the brace of trout resting on a broad palmetto leaf, and smiled. 'I see you can.'

Nathan expelled his breath on a long sigh. 'You must be Cole's wife,' he said, and she wondered why he looked so rueful when he said it. She didn't flatter herself that she was the reason for his discontent. But his tone was intriguing, and she determined to get to the bottom of it.

So, 'Yes,' she agreed, holding out her hand towards him. 'I'm Joanna Macallister. Who're you?'

His hesitation was only noticeable because she was aware of it. 'Nathan,' he said, after a moment. 'Nathan—Smith.' He shook her hand with some reluctance, and she wondered why. 'But I wish you wouldn't tell anyone you'd seen me here.'

Joanna frowned. 'Because of the fish?' she exclaimed. 'Oh, I'm sure——'

'Because I shouldn't be on the property,' Nathan cut in swiftly. 'I know it's asking a lot, but I'd appreciate it.'

Joanna blinked. 'You don't work for my husband or his father, then?'

'No.'

'But you know them. You knew I was Cole's wife.'

'Everyone knows that,' replied Nathan drily. Then, with a rueful glance about him, 'I think I'd better go.'

Joanna caught her lip between her teeth. 'Not on my account,' she protested. 'I won't tell anyone you were here.' She grimaced, remembering. 'There's no one to tell. Cole's away, and I'm not exactly on the best of terms with his mother and father.'

Nathan hesitated. 'Look, you don't know me. You don't know anything about me.' He pulled a wry face. 'I could be a murderer or a rapist, for all you know.'

Joanna regarded him consideringly. 'You have an honest face,' she said, and then, seeing the faint smile that tilted the corners of his mouth, she added, 'I'm prepared to take the risk, if you are. Why don't you show me what you were doing? Perhaps I could learn to catch fish, too.'

And that was how she and Nathan had become friends, she brooded painfully. A chance meeting, and suddenly she was embroiled in a situation she hadn't even known existed. Would Nathan still be alive, if she hadn't persuaded him to stay? It was entirely possible. But Nathan's life had always been in jeopardy, long before she came on the scene.

Still, in the months that followed, they did become close friends. He was interested in her painting, and encouraged her not to neglect her talent. And she found his knowledge of the area's history both informative and fascinating, and she was not at all surprised to learn that he taught at the Baptist school in Beaumaris.

But, these superficial facts aside, she learned very little about his personal life. He told her he was unmarried, and lived with his widowed mother in Beaumaris, but that was all. He wouldn't talk about the Macallisters, or why a feud should exist between them. He spoke of Cole, and Joe, and Ben, but they were not friends of his. If he had any friends, she never heard about them, and because she was lonely, too, she accepted his isolation quite gratefully.

At this time, her relationship with Cole was deteriorating rapidly. She didn't know why, but since his return from Argentina her husband had become increasingly remote. She knew he resented the fact that she had started sketching again, but it was more than that. And whenever she broached the subject of moving into a home of their own his only answer was that the plantation house was big enough for all of them.

It was certainly big enough for him to continue sleeping in a separate bedroom, she reflected bitterly, remembering the arguments they had about that. Cole's only excuse was that as he got up early in the morning and went to bed much later than she did at night he didn't want to disturb her. But Joanna guessed it was his mother's and father's idea. Another way to keep them apart.

A continuing source of conflict was Joanna's failure to conceive. Cole might occupy a different room, but he still came to her bed several times a week. She suspected it was a weakness he wished he could conquer, and because he could be so mean to her at other times she sometimes fought against his possession. But he always overcame her efforts. The feverish mating of their bodies had lost none of its fervour; it was totally obsessive to both of them, and even Cole couldn't deny the hunger in his blood.

Nevertheless, as the months went by and she didn't get pregnant, Cole became suspicious. Obviously his doubts had been fuelled by the things his parents im-

plied, and she found him one day searching her bedside drawers for contraceptives. Her anger at finding
him there was overwhelming, and more than erased any
advantage she might have gained because his search
had proved unsuccessful. But his parting comment,
that she probably hid them somewhere else, was the
final straw. That night, she locked her door against
him, refusing to answer when he hammered on the
panels. She even locked the balcony doors and closed
the shutters, preferring the airless atmosphere to the
shameful demands of her flesh.

Looking back now, she saw how foolishly she had
played into Ryan Macallister's hands. Cole was a proud
man. He wouldn't beg her to unlock her door. What
had begun as an angry revolt against his lack of faith
in her quickly accelerated into a full-blown separa-
tion. In a matter of days, she and Cole were acting like
strangers around one another. And, before she could
pluck up the courage to speak to him, something happened that altered her mind irrevocably.

The past few months might not have been the most
happy time in her life, but she had always believed that,
because she and Cole still had such a good sexual relationship, sooner or later their problems would be re-
solved. If she hadn't believed that, she couldn't have
continued in the marriage. But Cole still loved her; she
was sure of it. And, in time, he would see it her way.

She had been given the use of an old station wagon,
mainly, she suspected, because it enabled her to take
the younger children to school, when no one else was
available. But it did give her a certain amount of freedom, and she and Charley often went into Beaumaris
at weekends, to potter about the small stores, and
watch the fishing boats coming and going from the

harbour. Of all the Macallisters, apart from Cole, she liked Charley best. The little girl had become her shadow since the incident in the spring, when Joanna had played such a crucial part in rescuing her from the island in the river, where they had been picnicking. Their row-boat had come adrift, and Joanna had had to swim to the shore to get help. It had been a near thing, and for a while afterwards she and Cole seemed to get close again. But subsequent events, particularly the incident over the contraceptives, had destroyed their understanding, and when Joanna drove into Beaumaris that Saturday morning she was still mulling over ways to make amends.

And then she saw Cole.

He was parked in the centre of town, right where she usually parked, leaning against the bonnet of the dust-smeared pick-up he invariably drove, laughing with a blonde in a hot pink jump-suit.

Joanna had thought he was exercising the horses with Ben. He had gone out earlier that morning, and that was what his mother had told her, when she had asked where he was. But it was obvious from his dress shirt and well-cut trousers that he had never had any intention of going riding.

'Hell!'

Charley's unguarded exclamation echoed the reaction Joanna was feeling. The girl was flirting with Cole now, finger-walking up his shirt, and arching her body towards him. There was a wealth of confidence and intimacy in her attitude, and Joanna's stomach hollowed at the obvious explanation.

But Charley's behaviour could at least provide her with half an answer. 'Who is she?' she asked stiffly, and Charley stifled a groan.

'Sammy-Jean Butler,' she muttered reluctantly, pursing up her face. 'Damn, what's he doing with *her*?'

Trying not to sound as sick as she felt, Joanna tried to make light of it. 'Who knows?' she said, stepping on the brakes, and turning the station wagon into a spot several yards from where her husband was standing. 'It looks as if they just ran into one another.' She wet her lips. 'Is she an old girlfriend?'

Charley hunched her shoulders. 'I guess.'

'Well, is she, or isn't she?'

Charley sniffed. 'Ma and Pa wanted Cole to marry her one time,' she admitted. 'See, the Butlers' place is next to Tidewater, and Pa and Mr Butler used to talk about how good it would be if Cole and Sammy-Jean...'

Joanna remembered how hard it had been for her to get out of the station wagon after that, to go and speak to her husband. And, when she found the pick-up wasn't there any more, she didn't know whether to be glad or sorry. But it served a bitter purpose. She knew she would never trust Cole again.

CHAPTER TEN

CHARLEY came to find Joanna as soon as she got home from school. Her knock at the bedroom door was reminiscent of other occasions, when the girl had spent more time with her sister-in-law than she did with the other members of her family. But in those days Joanna had sought comfort from her. Now, it was Charley who needed commiseration.

'Donna's a bitch!' she declared, after Joanna had let her into the bedroom and resumed drying her hair in front of the mirror. 'Twins are supposed to support one another, aren't they?' Her jaw jutted. 'She just enjoys causing me aggravation!'

Joanna turned off the drier, and regarded her visitor with sympathetic eyes. 'Cool down,' she said. 'It's too hot to get so riled up over anything. What did Donna do, for heaven's sake? Steal your boyfriend?'

'Worse than that!' exclaimed Charley, flinging herself down on the end of the bed, and staring broodingly at the carpet. 'She's just gone and told Ma that Billy and me are going steady.'

'Oh.' Joanna wrapped the silk dressing-gown she had slipped on after her shower closer about her slim figure. 'I see.'

'Is that all you can say?' cried Charley, her eyes wide and indignant. 'Ma's grounded me for the next month, and she says if I try to see Billy again she'll get Pa to throw him out of Palmer's Point.'

Joanna's mouth tightened. Ryan Macallister was good at that, she thought contemptuously. He was good at destroying people's lives. Look what he'd done to Sarah!

'Did you talk with Cole yet?' Charley was asking now, and Joanna put her own grievances aside to answer the girl.

She shook her head. 'Charley, I only arrived yesterday.'

'Did you talk to Pa, then? Did he tell you why he wanted to see you?'

'I've spoken to him, yes.'

'And?'

Joanna sighed. 'Charley, I'd rather not talk about that right now.' She paused, and then added, 'Look, I will tell Cole what's happened. But I can't make any promises.'

Charley pushed herself up from the bed. 'You won't need to *tell* Cole,' she muttered. 'Leave it to Ma to do that. I just hoped you'd had a chance to talk with him before it all came out. Damn, what am I going to do? I love Billy. I can't give him up.'

Joanna moved to put her arm around the girl. 'Don't lose heart,' she said. And then, because she understood only too well how Charley was feeling, she went on, 'As I say, I can't promise anything, but there might be something I can do. Leave it with me. And don't you do anything stupid.'

'I won't.' Charley gazed at her hopefully. 'I saw the way Cole was looking at you last night. He's still stuck on you, isn't he? Gee, no wonder Sammy-Jean never stood a chance.'

'What do you mean?'

Joanna knew she shouldn't have asked the question, but she simply couldn't help it, and Charley smirked. 'Come on,' she said. 'I heard Ben telling you, things haven't been the same around here since you walked out.'

'Oh.' Joanna wondered why she suddenly felt so deflated. 'Well, as I say, I'll do what I can about you and Billy. Now, I think you'd better go. I've got to get ready for dinner.'

Tonight, Joanna decided to wear loose-fitting silk cut-offs that allowed the air to flow freely around her legs. They were tan, and combined attractively with the cream and gold box jacket she chose to wear with them. The jacket had a high neck, with an upstanding Chinese collar, and because of its brevity it occasionally exposed an inch of olive skin around her midriff. Her earrings were gold again, beaten squares of metal that accentuated the slenderness of her neck. And she swept her hair up into a loose knot, allowing several strands of midnight silk to droop beside her ears.

To her surprise, the library was empty when she went down. Of course, she was a little earlier than the night before, and it was possible she was the only person dining at home. Apart from Cole's father, of course, but there was no guarantee that he would join her. In any event, Joanna decided to help herself to a drink. She'd had nothing but tap water since lunchtime, and she felt she needed some stimulant to get her through the evening ahead. Even if she had to spend it alone, she consoled herself grimly. There was something about this place that always put her nerves on edge.

The drinks cabinet had been replenished, after the night before, and her hand hovered over the whiskey for a moment, before moving on to the wine. Better she keep her wits about her, just in case, she thought drily. No one was going to accuse her of over-imbibing these days.

She was raising the glass of wine to her lips when she realised she was no longer alone. While she had been concentrating on not spilling any of the wine over the polished surface of the cabinet, Cole had come to stand in the doorway. With his shoulder propped against the jamb, he was watching her actions with narrowed eyes, and when Joanna became aware of him she felt a moment's regret.

He looked so attractive standing there, his hair damp and still clinging to his head after his shower. The water had darkened its silvery-blond strands, casting an artificial shadow across his face, and, in spite of the fact that he had shaved, a glistening of bristle lay over his jawline. He was wearing navy trousers and a roll-necked cotton sweater in a lighter shade of blue. The heat never seemed to bother him, Joanna reflected, but of course he was used to it. And then, part of the heat she was feeling was self-induced, brought on by the unwilling memory of her thoughts that afternoon.

'All alone?' she enquired, going on the old adage that it was easier to attack than defend. 'Can I get you a drink?' She held up her glass. 'The wine's very good. I can recommend it.'

Cole said nothing, but he straightened from his lounging position and came across the room towards her. However, although her skin prickled, and all her pulses set up a wild tattoo, he didn't touch her. Instead, he lifted the bourbon bottle and poured himself a generous measure over ice, swallowing a mouthful before acknowledging her comments.

He smelt good, too, she noticed, the scent of the soap he had been using drifting to her nostrils. She could even smell the heat of his skin, clean, and faintly musky, and incredibly masculine...

God! She brought herself up there, forcing herself to remember where she was. As the realisation of what she was thinking—and what it was doing to her—swept over her in mindless waves, she saw the yawning pit she was digging for herself. He was her ex-husband, for pity's sake! Not someone of critical importance in her life. And she had come to know his scent as well as her own, so—big deal! She could live with that. She took a breath. She had to.

'We'll be dining alone,' he said, as she struggled to assume a casual demeanour, and she wondered whose idea that was. Not his mother's, she was sure. Maggie would never condone such a suggestion.

'I see,' she murmured, her brows arching inquisitively, and, as if sensing a sarcasm she was far from feeling, Cole went on,

'Yes.' He paused. 'Ma, Sandy and the twins are having supper at Joe's. And—Ben has a date this evening.'

'Really?' Giving herself time to think, Joanna took another sip of wine. 'I thought Charley was grounded.'

Cole frowned. 'Grounded?'

Joanna considered quickly. She had no wish to involve Charley yet. Not until she had had a chance to sound out the situation. 'I—it's not important,' she said. Then, tilting her head, 'Will your father be joining us?'

'Not tonight.' Cole's mouth compressed, and he turned to pour more bourbon into his glass.

'Oh?' Joanna moistened her lips. 'Why not? He's not——'

'Worse?' Cole swung around, cradling his glass between his strong fingers. 'Do you care?'

Joanna endeavoured to remain unmoved. 'I hardly think your mother would be spending the evening at Joe's, if he was in any danger,' she replied smoothly, and Cole assumed an irritated expression.

'No,' he said after a moment. 'No, you're right, of course. He's no worse and no better than he was. But——' the word was heavy with meaning '—he thinks it would be a good idea if we—talked to one another.'

Now Joanna understood. But, 'Talked?' she queried, with just the right amount of confusion in her voice. 'What about?'

Cole's jaw hardened. 'What do you think?'

'I don't know, do I?'

He grunted. 'He wants us to—reconcile——'

'Reconcile!' Now Joanna couldn't keep the disbelief out of her voice. 'You mean, he wants us to get together again?'

'No!' Cole swore. 'Not that. He's ill, but he's not senile!' He expelled his breath on a harsh sigh. 'No, he simply wants us to try and heal our differences; to be—civil—with one another again.'

Joanna stared at him. 'Why?'

'Why?' Cole had obviously thought of this himself, but he didn't have an answer for her. 'I—why do you think? He's sick. Near to death. People who are dying sometimes have these crazy ideas. I guess he wants to—to——'

'Salve his own conscience?' suggested Joanna silkily, and Cole's face suffused with angry colour.

'You would say that, wouldn't you?' he snarled. 'I should have known better than to hope you'd show some compassion.'

Joanna shrugged. 'Maybe you should,' she agreed, putting down her glass. She had suddenly lost all taste for the wine. 'Or perhaps you should learn to have some compassion yourself.'

'What's that supposed to mean?'

Joanna hesitated. 'You haven't asked me why your father wanted to see me.'

Cole's mouth flattened. 'I know why. I've just told you why.'

'No, you haven't.'

He scowled. 'Stop bulling me, Jo. You know damn well how hard this is for me—for both of us. Don't—don't make it any worse by lying about it.'

Joanna felt a moment's indignation, but it passed. 'I'm not lying,' she said. 'Your father doesn't care if we hate each other's guts! My God, he and your mother did what they could to bring that about. Why should he feel any differently now? I'm still the foreigner! The outsider! The unwanted intruder, who spoiled all the plans your daddy had for you!'

'That's history, Jo. Let it go. It's not as if you made any attempt to fit in here. I don't remember you doing much else but moan about this place. You didn't like the way we lived, the way we treated the workers, the lack of health care on the estate.' He shook his head. 'No, all you did was cause trouble.'

'My, oh, my!' Joanna brought her hands together in a slow clap. 'You're learning, Cole. I could almost believe that was your daddy talking.'

'Shut up!'

'No. Why should I?' Joanna was keeping her anger in check by a supreme effort. 'It's the truth. Tell me, when are you Macallisters going to realise this is the twentieth century?'

Cole took a step towards her, but, whatever his intentions had been, the appearance of a maid, to inform them that supper was waiting, forestalled him.

'Right, Sally, we'll be right there,' he muttered, and, swallowing the remainder of the whiskey in his glass, he gestured for Joanna to precede him out of the room. And she did so, uneasily aware of her ex-husband's grim presence behind her.

Supper was served in a high-ceilinged salon, where a pair of revolving fans endeavoured to keep the air circulating. It was where they had all eaten the night before, but this evening only two places were set at the long polished table. Predictably, Cole sat in the chair his father had occupied the night previously, with Joanna at his right hand. It was nearer than she would have liked, but at least they weren't sitting opposite one another. She didn't know how she would have coped with such an unguarded appraisal.

As it was, she endeavoured to concentrate on her food, and her surroundings, to the exclusion of all else. She needed time to consider how she was going to proceed, and it didn't help that Cole had his own preconceived ideas of why she was here. The trouble was, she didn't know what she was going to do. She had forgotten how it was here. Somehow, the heat sapped her powers of reasoning. What had appeared so cut and dried in Nassau no longer seemed so easy.

Looking at him out of the corners of her eyes, as he attacked the chunky fish soup, and quail stuffed with cornbread, she wondered why she didn't just tell Ryan

Macallister to do his own dirty work, and get out of there. She didn't want to stay. And it was obvious Cole didn't want her here. She didn't owe his father anything. Nothing good, at least.

'Do you ever see Sarah?' she asked abruptly, knowing it would antagonise him, but reckless none the less. Anything to rid herself of this feeling that she was weakening. She had to remember exactly what he'd done.

Cole put down his fork, and reached for the glass of wine beside his plate. 'Why?' he asked, after rinsing his palate. 'What relevance does that have to this situation?'

Joanna bit her lip. 'I'd like to know if she's all right.'

'She is.'

'And Henry?'

'I've told you. Henry still works in the stables.'

Joanna shook her head. 'How can he?'

'How can't he? He still has to live. He earns enough to keep himself and his mother at Tidewater.'

'Conscience money!'

She was scathing, and a nerve jerked in Cole's cheek. 'May I remind you that Henry worked at Tidewater long before you knew anything about his brother? He likes the work. He's good with horses.'

'There are other places——'

'Not for someone like Henry,' retorted Cole savagely. 'For God's sake, what would you have us do? Deprive him of his chance to have some self-respect? If, as you say, you think it's conscience money, think about how he'd live if he didn't come to Tidewater. In any case, it's what Sarah wants. Now, will you give it a rest?'

Joanna took a steadying breath. 'Why don't you want me to see Sarah?'

Cole closed his eyes for a moment. 'Why do you think?'

'I don't know, do I? I'm asking you.'

Cole hesitated. 'All right. In words of one syllable, she doesn't want to see you.'

Joanna gasped. 'I don't believe you.'

'Nevertheless, it's the truth.'

Joanna shook her head. 'I don't understand.'

'Try. Your presence here can only bring back unhappy memories for her.'

'It does?' Joanna winced. 'Does she—does she hate me?'

'No!' Cole was impatient. 'Sarah doesn't hate anyone.'

'Not even your father?'

'Not even him,' declared Cole flatly. 'You know Sarah. She doesn't have a vindictive bone in her body. Now—why don't you stop thinking everyone's your enemy, and try and enjoy your time here?'

Joanna licked her lips. 'With you, you mean?' she ventured, her pulses suddenly racing, and Cole's expression tightened.

'If that's what it takes,' he said guardedly. 'I brought you here. I guess I have to take my share of the responsibility.'

'Gee, thanks.'

Joanna was sarcastic, but she still couldn't control the quickening rate of her heartbeat. A few days with Cole, she mused, with some nervousness. Was that what she really wanted? What she could handle? And was she going to plead his father's case, or was she going to allow him to go on thinking that all his father wanted was some cosy reconciliation?

Cole had picked up his fork again, but, from the way he was pushing the meat and peas around his plate, food was the last thing on his mind. After a few moments, he threw the fork down again, and wiped his mouth on his napkin.

'Tomorrow,' he said, and she knew the words were being dragged out of him, 'tomorrow, we'll take a ride out to Palmer's Point.' He paused. 'There's something you might like to see.'

'What?' Joanna's eyes were curious.

'You'll find out,' he said, pushing back his chair, and getting up from the table. 'Now, if you'll excuse me, I have work to do.'

'Work?' Joanna looked sceptically towards the inky darkness outside, where fireflies and huge, hairy moths clustered against the window-pane. 'What work?'

'Paperwork,' Cole informed her briefly, nodding to the maid to come and clear. 'Someone has to run Tidewater, now that my father isn't able to do it. Mary-Lou will get you anything else you want. I'll see you in the morning.'

He was walking towards the door when another thought occurred to her. Turning her head, she said, 'Cole!' and, with a perceptible stiffening of his shoulders, he halted in the doorway.

'Yes?'

'What time in the morning?' she asked innocently, twining a strand of silky dark hair about her fingers as she spoke, and Cole's eyes narrowed.

'Seven,' he stated harshly, slapping one hand against the jamb, and, without waiting for any response, he strode out of the room.

Joanna was walking along the upper corridor to her room when she heard a whispering sound behind her. For a moment, it unnerved her. She hadn't heard a door open, or anyone call her name, and because the lamps that lit the landing were few, and inclined to flicker, she knew a moment's panic. The old house was like that. Boards creaked; shutters banged; and just occasionally the electricity failed altogether.

She swung round, half prepared to face whatever demon was pursuing her, and then caught her breath at the sight of Ryan Macallister, following her in his wheelchair.

'Did I scare you?' he asked, in a low voice, and she knew damn well he knew he had. But she refused to give him that satisfaction.

'Is that how you get your kicks these days, Mr Macallister?' she asked, keeping her voice steady and adopting a provocative stance. She tipped her head, and rested one hand on her hip. 'And here I was thinkin' y'all had turned over a new leaf!'

If her words, and the way they were delivered, angered him, he did an admirable job of hiding his feelings. Instead, he wheeled himself closer, so that if she had chosen to stretch out her leg she could have touched the foot-rest. Then, looking up into her guarded features, he demanded, 'Did you do it?'

Joanna took a step back. It was an involuntary movement, an automatic recoil from the avidity of his expression. He didn't frighten her, but he did disturb her, and tonight she was in no state to counter his belligerence.

'Did I do what?' she responded now, guessing that pretending ignorance was the only way to thwart him.

'I had dinner with Cole, if that's what you mean. You should have joined us. The quail was——'

'Goddammit, don't mess with me, girl!' Ryan's voice rose in concert with his fury, and he cast an impatient glance over his shoulder. Then, calming himself with an evident effort, he added harshly, 'You know what I'm talking about. Did you talk to him? Did you tell him what I told you?'

'We've talked.' Joanna thought about prevaricating, but she found she didn't have the energy—or the enthusiasm. 'That's all I can tell you.'

'What about?' Ryan's jaw clamped.

'This and that.' Joanna sighed. 'Now, if you don't mind, I'd like to go into my room. I'm tired.'

'Dammit, I know you and Cole talked about Nathan,' Ryan blustered angrily. 'Hannibal heard you asking about Henry, and Cole saying something about Sarah not blaming anyone for Nathan's death——'

'You had Hannibal spy on us?' broke in Joanna disbelievingly, her disgust at the act tempered by her sympathy for Ryan's elderly valet. Hannibal had been at Tidewater since before Ryan was born, and his loyalty to his employer had never been in doubt.

'Not all the time,' muttered Cole's father irritably, but there was no remorse in the words. 'The old fool's half deaf anyway. But don't you try to bluff me, girl. I always know what's going on in this house.'

'Then you won't need me to tell you, will you?' retorted Joanna shortly, and, thrusting open her door, she slammed into the room.

CHAPTER ELEVEN

JOANNA half thought he might try to follow her, but he didn't. Even though she lay back against the closed panels for several minutes, ready to resist if he should try to force his way inside, there was no further intrusion. Evidently Cole's father had decided he had said enough for one night. He had startled her, and attempted to intimidate her, and finally told her she was being spied on. What else could he do?

When she eventually pushed herself away from the door, her movements were heavy and lethargic. It was all very well putting up a defiant front with the Macallisters, but there was no doubt it drained her emotionally. She had to be constantly alert, constantly on her guard. What a holiday, she reflected ruefully. She'd have had less stress white-water-rafting in the Rockies!

She undressed wearily, and after sluicing her face in the bathroom she crawled into bed. She just wanted to forget all about Cole and his family and go to sleep. Maybe tomorrow things would be clearer. Maybe tomorrow she'd find a reason for being here.

But sleep eluded her. She tossed and turned for hours, and eventually had to get up to go to the bathroom. Peering at her pale face in the mirror above the washbasin as she rinsed her hands, she bemoaned the fact that she was going to look an absolute hag in the morning—when Cole took her riding to Palmer's Point.

She frowned. Why there? she brooded. The shacks at Palmer's Point had always been a bone of contention between them. And it was hardly a beauty spot, although it did overlook the mouth of the Tidewater River. It was where the Smiths had lived, before Adam died, and Ryan Macallister found Sarah and her two sons a house in Beaumaris. And it was while Sarah was living at Palmer's Point that Ryan first noticed her.

Nathan's mother had been beautiful when Joanna knew her, and it didn't take much imagination to realise that at eighteen she must have been quite ravishing. With her sloe-dark eyes, and her tall, statuesque figure, she must have presented quite a challenge to the arrogant master of Tidewater.

Sarah and Adam had been married for three years, and their son, Henry, had been two years old, when Ryan first started taking an unnatural interest in the Smiths. Henry was already showing signs of slowness, of not being as bright as the other children who lived in the shacks, and Ryan used the boy's disability as a reason for visiting the family. He arranged for the boy to see a specialist, and insisted on escorting Sarah into Charleston himself. And he paid for the child to attend a special school, so that Henry could have a real chance of leading a normal life.

Of course, his reasons were not philanthropic. Ryan Macallister never did anything for anyone without demanding payment. And, although Sarah knew that what she was doing was wrong, she couldn't help being flattered by the older man's attentions. Besides, she consoled herself with the knowledge that he was helping Henry, and only when she found herself pregnant with the other man's child did the fear of how her husband would react when he found out compel her to confront Ryan with her dilemma.

To Ryan, the answer was simple. She must get rid of the baby. He would give her the money to have an abortion. He knew of a woman in Charleston who would do the deed, with no questions asked.

Sarah refused. She was hurt and anxious, but nothing would persuade her to do away with her baby. She would have the child, she said, and if Adam disowned her, so be it. She would get a job and support both her children. She would survive.

But something happened that made her worries about her pregnancy merely academic. Adam was killed—in a freak accident in the fields. He was run down by a mechanical picker, and in her grief at losing the man she had lived with for more than three years Sarah was once again vulnerable to Ryan's persuasion.

It was fairly easy for him to convince her that she wouldn't be happy, staying in the shack, which must contain so many upsetting memories. Instead, he set her up in a house in Beaumaris—far enough from Tidewater so that when her baby was born no one would associate it with him, and near enough so that he could continue to visit her on a regular basis.

Nathan had told Joanna this, when, heartbroken over Cole's behaviour, she had gone to him for support. Nathan had been the only person she could discuss Cole's unfaithfulness with. And, whether to comfort her, or to expunge some of the bitterness he still possessed, she never knew, but he told her the whole, unhappy story.

Joanna had been shocked, but not as shocked as she might have been before learning of Cole's unfaithfulness. And, in the weeks that followed, he took her to meet his mother, and she learned more. She discovered that Ryan still occasionally visited the house in Acacia Street. She discovered that in all these years Margaret Macallister had remained unaware of Nathan's existence. She learned that her father-in-law lived two distinct lives: one at Tidewater Plantation, and the other with his mistress in Beaumaris.

She didn't blame Sarah. Nathan's mother was one of life's victims. Joanna had no doubt that when Ryan first affected an interest in Henry Sarah had taken his kindness at face value. She must have been flattered that her son had been singled out for attention, and, having seen the shacks at Palmer's Point, Joanna could understand her dilemma.

It was through talking to Sarah that Joanna eventually visited the shacks for herself. Nathan went with her, and, although at first the women were suspicious of her, gradually she won their confidence. To begin with, it was just something to do, somewhere to go when Cole was working or away from the plantation. She took her sketch pad with her, and spent hours producing likenesses of the children for their mothers. She talked to the children, and encouraged them to talk to her. And, in time, their mothers began to trust her, telling her their problems, and asking her advice.

She supposed it had been a gigantic step from there to actually starting the mother and baby clinic, but so many of the women had had children who'd died, and others were weary from so many pregnancies. Health care was expensive, and Joanna, who would have loved a baby of her own, whatever Cole thought to the contrary, was more than eager to help. Some of the older women, who were past child-bearing themselves, but who wanted a better life for their daughters, helped too. A derelict shack was appropriated, and between them they repaired and painted the inside, and hung the posters Joanna had provided. There were scales to weigh the babies, and a creaky old couch, where the mothers were examined. Her biggest coup was in persuading the hospital in Beaumaris to offer the services of a doctor, free of charge, one afternoon a week, to provide the medical skills necessary for the clinic to succeed.

It was ironic, she thought, that, while she was so successful in helping other people, she was so unsuccessful in helping herself. Her marriage had failed. She and Cole seldom spoke to one another any more. Oh, she supposed, if she had been willing to overlook his involvement with Sammy-Jean, they might have been able to work something out. If she had been willing to humble herself, and beg him to come back to her. But she had her pride, and she refused to barter it, even though sometimes the need to touch him was like a raging ache inside her.

And then, one afternoon, Cole came to the clinic and found Nathan helping her. Joanna had known he was aware of the clinic's existence. His father knew about it, and he had sworn he would get the place closed down. He objected to his daughter-in-law being involved, and he had told Cole to deal with it. But, as she and Cole rarely had a conversation these days, nothing had happened, and as the weeks went by she had cautiously begun to hope they were safe.

Cole's appearance had destroyed that hope. She had been convinced he could have no other reason for coming to the clinic than to do his father's bidding. That was why she had jumped recklessly into the attack, accusing him of being his father's lackey, and ordering him off the premises.

In retrospect, she could see it had been the wrong thing to do. She had immediately created a volatile situation, and the row that had ensued had been every bit as violent as she had anticipated. And, when Nathan sprang to her defence, things got really ugly.

Even today, it was hard to understand Cole's fury towards Nathan. Rounding on the younger man, he had delivered one of the most abusive speeches of his entire life. He had accused Nathan of every crime he could think of, finishing with a warning that he should stay away from Macallister women and off Macallister land.

And that was when Joanna had told him. Ignoring Nathan's warning hand on her sleeve, she had informed Cole exactly who Nathan was. His name might be Smith, she said icily, but that wasn't the name of his father. His father's name was Macallister, just like his. In fact, he was speaking to his brother.

Cole had been stunned. Looking back now, she had to admit that, of all the Macallisters, Cole had taken it the hardest. For, of course, he had confronted his father with the accusation, and other ears had heard Ryan's angry outburst. The news had spread like wildfire, and what had just been a rumour became a verified fact.

Maggie Macallister showed little reaction, proving, to Joanna at least, that Cole's mother must have known what was happening all along. But, as long as it wasn't talked about, and Ryan was discreet, she had been prepared to ignore it. After all, Nathan was twenty-one. She must have thought the worst was over.

And it might have been, if Ryan had been prepared to leave it there. After all, it wasn't such an unusual story. Without further scandal to feed on, the story would have been nothing more than a nine-day wonder. But Ryan was angry. He wanted retribution. And, because it was Joanna who had betrayed him, he chose to use her to get his revenge.

The first that Joanna knew about it was when she next went into Beaumaris to see Sarah. Although she knocked at the door of the house in Acacia Street, no one answered, and when she went to the clinic, seeking Nathan, she found the shack had been bulldozed to the ground. And none of the women wanted to talk to her. They were cool, and offhand, avoiding her eyes when she tried to get them to tell her what had happened, calling their children away, as if she was to blame for everything.

She knew it was Ryan Macallister who was behind it. She could imagine the threats he had made not just to these women, but to Sarah as well. Was that why Sarah wasn't answering her door? Was that why Nathan was avoiding her?

She thought about going to the school where Nathan taught, and asking him what he thought she should do, but the trouble was, she felt guilty. After all, if she hadn't betrayed Sarah's confidence, none of this would have happened. It was her fault that it had all gone wrong. Her fault that all her hard-earned efforts were wasted.

She knew there was only one person she could appeal to, and that was Cole. She hadn't spoken to him once since that day at the clinic, but somehow she had to make him see that it wasn't fair to punish others for her mistakes. Nathan was such an honourable man. It wasn't right that he should have to suffer for simply being there. He hadn't asked to be born. He hadn't chosen his parents.

She went to Cole's room that night, long after his parents had gone to bed. She knew it was the only time when she might get to speak to him alone, but her hands were trembling as she tied the cord of the silk wrapper around her. Her appearance didn't please her. Since she and Cole had been living separate lives, she had piled on the weight, and her hips swelled unattractively below the belt of the robe. Her breasts were bigger, too, round and voluptuous, bouncing along beneath the wrapper like two melons in a bag.

But, although she spent several minutes trying to attract Cole's attention, he didn't open the door. And, when she eventually plucked up the courage to step inside, she found the room was empty. The maid had turned down the bed, but it hadn't been occupied.

She was debating whether to go back to her own room, when she heard a sound behind her. Cole had evidently just arrived home, and was standing in the doorway, swaying slightly on his heels.

'Well, well,' he said unpleasantly, 'to what do I owe this honour? Or is it a case of if Mohammed won't come to the mountain, the mountain must come to Mohammed?'

His voice was slightly slurred, as if he had been drinking. But the words he used were deliberate, and Joanna coloured. 'I wanted to talk to you, Cole,' she said, wishing now she had waited till the morning. 'I— but it doesn't matter.'

However, when she would have gone past him, he stepped inside and closed the door. 'Go ahead,' he said. 'I'm listening. You'll sleep better if you spit it out. They say that confession's good for the soul!'

'Confession?'

Joanna was confused, but Cole merely unfastened the remaining buttons on his shirt and pulled it free of his trousers. 'Sure,' he said, tossing his jacket aside and running exploring fingers across his chest. 'You're going to tell me how sorry you are for making a fool of me with Nathan. Tell me about it. I hear he's pretty impressive in that department. Got all the right equipment, if you see what I mean——'

'Shut your filthy mouth!'

Joanna's hand swung towards his cheek with all the force she could muster, but Cole only swayed back on his heels and avoided the worst of the blow. Besides, he was probably anaesthetised against any pain by the amount of alcohol he had swallowed, she thought bitterly. Unlike her.

'Hey, that's what they say,' Cole protested, his lean features showing only a mocking disregard for her anger. 'Don't blame me if he's found someone else!'

Joanna seethed. 'He hasn't found anyone else!' she exclaimed, frustratedly. 'That is, our—our relationship wasn't like that!'

'Oh, come on, Jo! I know what a hot little body you've got. And if you're not cooling it with me...' He shrugged expressively.

Joanna gasped. 'Is that all you can think about? *Sex*?'

Cole's face sobered. 'What else is there?' he asked harshly.

Joanna winced. 'I thought we loved one another——'

'Oh, spare me that!' Cole was scathing. 'You don't love me. You never did. All you love are those bloody paintings of yours! They're your family, aren't they? Your children! When we got married, I thought you'd forget all about that nonsense. I thought you'd be so busy having my babies, you wouldn't have time to think about anything else. But that's not what you had in mind. Children are a nuisance. They'd get in the way of your work. And heaven help anything that interfered with that!'

Joanna stared at him. 'You actually expected me to have children here? In this house?'

'Why not? You never gave my family a chance. You were so busy finding reasons for not living here, you didn't see what you were doing to us!'

'I didn't do anything to *us*! I wasn't the one who moved out of our room. I wasn't the one who went off to South America for weeks at a time, so that when you came back we were like strangers with one another.'

'And whose fault was that?'

'Well, it wasn't mine——'

'Not even when I found out what was going on?'

Joanna blinked. 'What *was* going on?'

'Do I have to spell it out?' Cole thrust his hands into his trouser pockets, and Joanna had to drag her eyes away from the taut cloth. 'We've been married over a year, Jo. Why aren't you pregnant?'

Joanna caught her breath. 'Perhaps you ought to ask yourself that,' she retorted indignantly. 'I takes two to make a baby, you know.'

Cole's eyes darkened. 'You bitch!'

'Oh, yes, I'm a bitch, aren't I? Just because I suggest that good 'ole Cole Macallister mightn't have what it takes——'

'Shut up!'

Cole reached for her then, and, although she tried to avoid his hands, he was less intoxicated than she had thought. His fingers fastened around her throat with bruising intent, and when he hauled her up in front of him her eyes opened wide with apprehension.

'You know what I should do, don't you?' he snarled. 'I should wring your lying little neck!'

'Because you can't take the truth?' Joanna taunted, scared, but defiant too, and Cole groaned.

'What the hell are you trying to do to me?' he demanded, his fingers finding her windpipe and exerting an unsteady pressure. 'God in heaven, you'd try the patience of a saint!'

'And we both know you're no saint, don't we?' whispered Joanna, through dry lips. 'Go on, Cole. Do it! Put us both out of our misery!'

Cole's hands tightened, and for a moment she thought he was going to make good his threat. And then they gentled, smoothing the skin of her throat, and tracing the pulsing veins that had risen, thread-like, to the surface. 'You know what I really want to do with you, don't you?' he muttered, his breath wafting across her face, only lightly tinged with the alcohol he had consumed. His hands slid down, over her quivering shoulders, and found the rampant fullness of her breasts. He squeezed them hard, through the slippery silk of her wrapper. Then he bent his head, and sucked one of the button-hard peaks into his mouth, suckling it through the cloth, and sending a wave of longing surging into her thighs.

She thought she was going to collapse, her knees felt so weak. But, as if sensing this, Cole put his hands beneath her bottom, and lifted her into his arms. Her legs curled automatically about him, and she wound her arms around his neck. The feel of his smooth skin felt so good beneath her hands, and when his tongue probed her lips she met it with her own.

'God, I want you!' He shrugged off his shirt, and his bare chest was unbelievably sensuous against her aching nipples. She wanted to tear off the wrapper, and rub herself against him. As it was, the damp cloth only sensitised her awareness of the masculine beauty of his body.

His tongue invaded her mouth, sliding across her teeth, and caressing the moist inner shell. Its greedy possession imitated the thrusting arousal of his body, and she could feel his swelling hardness rising beneath her hip.

When he carried her to the bed, and came down on top of her, she stopped trying to analyse what was happening. Perhaps he was doing this because he hated her. Perhaps he was using her to assuage his lust for Sammy-Jean. But she didn't care. What he was doing to her was what she wanted him to do to her, and the reasons for his urgency didn't really count. She wanted him—on her, and in her, melding their bodies together, and bringing her to a peak of fulfilment only he could achieve. She wanted to hold his sleek length inside her, the fullness of him stretching not just her muscles, but the limits of her consciousness. And she wanted to feel the liquid heat of his seed, lubricating the dryness of her soul.

And he was hungry for her. Of that, there could be no doubt. To her relief, the silk wrapper was quickly thrown aside, and his teeth tugged painfully at her nipple, as his hands fumbled awkwardly with his buckle. She wanted to help him, but he wouldn't let her. Instead, he dealt with his own belt and zip, while his mouth roamed freely over her flesh.

'Watch me,' he ordered once, when her drifting senses caused her eyes to close. 'Look at me!' And she did, as he nudged her thighs apart, and poised, erect and glistening above her. Then, groaning with satisfaction, he eased himself into her tight sheath, allowing her muscles to close about him with an eagerness she couldn't hide.

It was a frantic loving, a desperate meeting of souls, whose only outward connection was through their bodies. Yet it was a spiritual blending, too, a magical experience, when the pounding desire of possession became an urgent invocation of the sublime.

The end came all too soon. Driven to the heights of passion, it was far too tempting to tumble over the brink. Cole wanted to prolong it. She knew that by the way he tried to pace himself. But with her legs around his waist, and the luscious beauty of her mouth luring him on, the needs she was creating were too powerful to subdue. Besides, the desire to reach that tantalising peak was dragging every ounce of strength from him, and when he felt her wild convulsions he couldn't prevent his own explosion. A shuddering wave of tension swept through him, and then he slumped heavily on top of her.

And it was while they were lying in the sweat-slick aftermath of their lovemaking that Cole's door opened. Until then, Joanna had scarcely been aware that the lamps were still on, or that anyone could come into the room and find them. Besides, it was so late.

She had believed everyone was in bed. But it was Cole's father who stood in the doorway, and for a moment she saw that his face was as shocked as her own.

Cole's reactions were slower, more lethargic—even defiant, Joanna admitted now. At his father's hoarse exclamation, he didn't immediately spring up from the bed, as she might have expected. Oh, no. He merely rolled on to his back beside her, and turned hooded eyes in his father's direction. 'What do you want?' he demanded tersely. 'We're trying to get some sleep.'

Now Joanna pushed herself away from the bathroom basin, and walked wearily into the bedroom. And, as she did so, she realised it was the first time she had actually recalled the exact words Cole had used to his father that night. What had come afterwards had been so horrible that she hadn't been able to think. And time, and the desire not to remember, had erased the whole scene from her mind.

For Ryan had come to tell his son that Nathan was dead. He had been pulled out of the river an hour before, and his mother had insisted that Cole's father should be informed. In addition to which, the sheriff wanted him to go down to the morgue right away, to identify the body. Sarah was too distraught to see her son right now, and Ryan had agreed to do it. But he wanted Cole to go with him. He needed his eldest son's support.

And Cole had gone, Joanna remembered, leaving her to pull herself together, and return to her own room in a daze of disbelief. Nathan dead! She couldn't believe it was true. And why had he died in the river? For God's sake, couldn't he swim?

Her mind skimmed over the awful events of the next few days. If she and Cole had ever had a chance of regaining what they had once had, Nathan's death had destroyed it. She couldn't help blaming him for the way he had treated his half-brother. And she positively despised Ryan for his selfishness and blatant lack of feeling.

And then, at the funeral, something even more dreadful happened, something that had Joanna packing her bags, and swearing she would never set foot on Tidewater land again. Sarah, racked with grief, and driven to the edge by her son's untimely demise, had accused Ryan Macallister of causing it. He had hounded her son, she said, ever since he discovered that Joanna and Nathan were friends. He had accused him of seducing his brother's wife, of taking revenge for his own unhappy circumstances by destroying his brother's marriage. And Joanna had encouraged him, Ryan had added. Like took to like, he had sneered, with a scathing reference to Joanna's dark colouring.

Of course, Ryan had denied it. Red-faced and blustering, angry, now, that he had submitted to his son's conviction that they should attend the funeral, he had lashed out at anyone who had argued with him. But Joanna had seen his guilt, and despised him for it. And despised Cole, too, for letting it happen to a man who had been so kind, so gentle, so totally lacking in the arrogance his father had in such abundance.

For months afterwards, long after she had returned to London, and resumed her life there, Joanna tortured herself with thoughts of Nathan on that night. She couldn't believe it had been an accident. She had seen him fishing in the river so many times, and she was sure he would never have drowned unless he hadn't wanted to live. And, of course, she had blamed herself, not only for exposing Ryan and causing him to turn on his son, but also for being the unwitting tool his father had used against him. She could never forgive Ryan. Never. The problem was, did she want to forgive his son?

CHAPTER TWELVE

IT WAS years since Joanna had been on a horse. She had learned to ride as a child, and, when she first went to live at Tidewater, she had occasionally ridden with Cole. But only occasionally. After her illness, and their subsequent estrangement, she had had no heart for such a pursuit. It would have seemed too much like pursuing him, and her pride had balked at the idea.

But, after a sleepless night spent reliving the past, she once again found herself in the saddle. Cole had had a beautiful pearl-grey mare readied for her, and the animal shifted a little nervously as Joanna settled herself on its back. She knew that horses, like other animals, could sense nervousness in humans, but in her case it wasn't fear of riding that upset her stomach. It was her unwilling awareness of the man riding beside her. And the uneasy realisation of how attracted to him she still was.

Not that Cole seemed aware of her. He appeared cool and detached, totally in control of his own destiny. Leather-clad thighs moulded the sides of the huge blood bay he was riding, and his booted feet rested confidently in the stirrups. He was wearing a cream shirt, opened down the front to allow whatever breeze there was to cool his skin, and a broad-brimmed hat tipped forward to shade his eyes.

He looked lean and hard, and intensely male, his relaxed hands resting on the reins, nevertheless exuding an unmistakable sense of power. Sometimes, seeing him like this, feeling what his sexuality was doing to her, Joanna wondered how they had ever drifted apart. But then she remembered Nathan, and Sammy-Jean, and her weakness became a hurtful core of indignation.

'You need a hat,' he informed her, appraising her outfit of pink cotton cut-offs and a loose-fitting man's shirt with some contempt. But what did he expect her to wear, for heaven's sake? she asked herself resentfully. She hadn't known when she flew out to the Bahamas that she would end up riding trail in South Carolina. 'You don't want to get heatstroke, do you?'

Joanna shrugged. 'I wouldn't have thought you'd care,' she countered, realising she mustn't let him guess how he disturbed her, and adopting an appealing smile. But Cole only swung down from the bay, and strode back into the stables.

He emerged a few moments later with a rather worn and spotted stetson, and jammed it on to the pommel in front of her. 'Put it on,' he ordered, grasping the bay's reins and resuming his seat in the saddle. 'It's not pretty, but it should serve the purpose.'

'Why, darlin', are you sayin' that ah'm pretty?' Joanna goaded him, examining the hat with some disdain, and Cole's mouth compressed.

'Do you need me to tell you that?' he retorted, skilfully turning the tables, and Joanna pulled a face at his back, as she reluctantly tried the hat for size.

It was a close fit, and it immediately dislodged the knot she had made of her hair for coolness. The silky strands came tumbling down about her shoulders, and, hearing her gasp of irritation, Cole glanced round.

'Having problems?' he enquired sardonically, and, refusing to give him the satisfaction, Joanna shook her head.

'Nothing I can't handle,' she said, bundling all her hair inside the stetson, and jamming it on her head. 'By the way, where's Henry? Or am I not allowed to say hello to him either?'

Cole managed not to utter the retort that was evidently trembling on his lips, and instead he kicked the bay into motion. 'Henry only works here afternoons,' he said, as Joanna hastily nudged the mare into following him. 'He helps his mother at the guest house mornings.'

Joanna blinked. 'The guest house?' she echoed. 'Sarah works at a guest house?'

'She *runs* a guest house,' Cole corrected her shortly. Ignoring her look of surprise, he cast an expert eye over her handling of the mare. 'You fit for a little cantering?'

Joanna's hands tightened on the reins. 'Anything you like,' she declared absently, still mulling over what he had said about Sarah, but when Cole gave the bay its head she was forced to put her thoughts on hold. She hadn't forgotten how to ride, but she was out of practice, and her thighs jarred uncomfortably as she tried to find the rhythm.

They crossed dew-soaked paddocks, where the scent of the grass rose pungently to her nostrils, into rustling woods, where the sun's rays filtered through the boughs. The mare's hoofs crunched on cones and rotting leaves, and caused a startled jack-rabbit to scoot across their path. Birds sang; bees buzzed around a hive of wild honey; and the moisture rose from the forest floor to soak her perspiring skin.

They emerged into fields that stretched towards other forests of oak and palmetto, rich agricultural land, extending into undulating hills. But, instead of cotton fields as far as the eye could see, Joanna saw acres given over to corn and cattle, and orchards of fruit trees, with the mist rising from them.

Cole reined in the bay to guide the animal between rows of sweet-sprouting sugar cane. Insects buzzed about them, making Joanna glad she had remembered to cover the most sensitive parts of her body, and also giving her a reason for wearing the disgusting hat. She was even glad she was on horseback, when she remembered the spiders that thrived in the cane fields. And every time one of the swaying stalks touched her sleeve she brushed away another imaginary horror.

It wasn't until they came out of the sugar cane that she realised where they were. She had been disorientated by the changes that had been made at Tidewater, and it was with some surprise that she saw they weren't far from where the shacks had been situated. She could hear the river, too, and her nerves tightened with remembered pain. Was Cole so insensitive? she wondered. Didn't he understand that this was the last place she wanted to see?

But Cole was already some distance away from her, the bay trotting across the rough turf that separated Tidewater from the cluster of dwellings at Palmer's Point. He didn't look back, and she had only two choices: either go with him, or go back to the house.

And, because the prospect of returning to the house was even less attractive to her, she urged the mare after him. But resentment built as they cantered down the slope, and she glimpsed the roofs of the buildings below them.

She scarcely noticed the river, as she kicked the mare into a gallop and overtook him. She paid no attention to the mud-flats, where she had once spent so many hours, sketching the many birds that came to feed there. She didn't even smell the salty tang of the ocean, or pause to admire the long white stretch of sand that edged the estuary. All she could think about was her own feelings, which reinforced her hostility towards him for bringing her here.

'Is this supposed to be some kind of sick joke?' she demanded, as she passed him, but Cole didn't answer. And then, as the ground levelled out, she saw the cluster of dwellings immediately ahead of her.

Her astonishment was swift and genuine. The village was still there, just as she remembered. But the shacks had disappeared. In their place stood modern tract housing, mostly one-storey buildings, erected on piles for maximum coolness.

'Some joke, hmm?' murmured Cole, his stirrup nudging her leg, and Joanna gave an involuntary start. She had been staring at the bright borders of stocks and pansies that edged the squares of turf in front of each property, and the evidence of cultivation in the tent-like growth of bean-poles at the back.

'Your father did this?' she exclaimed, finding it difficult to associate the man she knew with what she was seeing in front of her, and Cole shrugged.

'Is that so hard to believe?'

'Frankly, yes.' Joanna shook her head. 'It's incredible!'

Cole expelled a long breath. 'Yeah, well...' He shook the reins and sent the bay walking down the dusty lane between the houses. 'As I said last night, I've got something to show you.'

'And this isn't it?'

Joanna was surprised, but Cole didn't answer her. Their arrival had attracted attention, and a woman had come out on to the veranda of the house opposite and called to him.

'Morning, there, Cole,' she said, resting her elbows on the rail, and smiling down at him. 'Somethin' I can do for you?'

'Morning, Susie,' Cole responded, as relaxed and easy as she was, and Joanna shook her head. It wasn't just the houses that had changed around here, she thought drily. And goodness, wasn't that Susan Fenton, Billy Fenton's mother?

'You remember Joanna, don't you?' Cole was saying now, and Susan turned a friendly smile on the other woman.

'Of course,' she said. 'Hi, there, Mrs Macallister. I heard you were back at Tidewater. Guess you didn't expect anythin' like this.'

'No.' Joanna managed a rueful grimace. 'How are you, Susan? You—er—you look well.'

And she did. Whether it was the fact that Joanna hadn't seen her for some time, she didn't know, but the woman looked fit and healthy, and undeniably pregnant. And much too attractive to be looking at Cole like that, Joanna acknowledged tensely. How well did he know her? Had he, like his father, found diversion here?

'Hey, I'm OK.' Susan propped her hip on the veranda rail, and rested a complacent hand on the swelling mound of her stomach. 'Never been better, as it happens. Since Cole moved us into these fancy houses, we all got no complaints.'

'Since Cole——' Joanna broke off and glanced at her ex-husband. 'Yes, I see.' She schooled her features. 'When's the baby due?'

'In a couple of months.' Susan grinned. 'You sure I can't get you anythin'? Some nice cold lemonade, maybe?'

'No, thanks.' Cole spoke before Joanna could say anything. 'You look after yourself, right? And don't let Jonas wear you out.'

Susan dimpled. 'I won't,' she said. 'See you later, Mrs Macallister. Y'all take care now.'

As they got out of earshot, Joanna nudged her horse nearer to Cole's. 'Jonas?' she said, frowning, and Cole pulled a wry face.

'Jonas Wilson,' he told her evenly. 'Her husband.'

'But I thought——'

'Bull's dead,' Cole intoned, acknowledging the greetings of several other women and children, who had come out on to their verandas to see what was going on. 'You've been away three years, Jo. Things change. People change.'

'Including your father?' she queried, tugging on the mare's reins, as a dusky-skinned little boy ran across her path. 'Hey, isn't that Georgie Davis? But no. It can't be.'

'Try his brother Bobby,' said Cole laconically, leaning across to grasp her bridle. 'I guess we walk from here. I'd hate for you to be the unwitting cause of someone's death.'

Joanna looked at him, but he wasn't looking her way, and, because their actions were being monitored by at least a dozen pairs of eyes, she hastily slid out of the saddle. But the significance of what he had said wasn't lost on her, and she wished he hadn't made such a statement right in the middle of Palmer's Point.

Their progress after that was slow. So many people wanted to stop, and pass the time of day. They were obviously curious about Joanna, but strangely enough she felt an outsider. Even though she knew most of these people, it wasn't the same. She had abandoned them, and Cole had taken her place.

Not that she really minded. She was glad Cole had found his own role at Tidewater. And she was truly delighted that she had played some small part in his enlightenment. She just wished he could have told her, before she ran away...

The direction her thoughts were taking her was suddenly frightening. She couldn't mean what she was thinking. Her relationship with Cole had floundered long before Nathan died. There was still Sammy-Jean, and her own inability to conceive. Besides, she had her work. She didn't want to come back to South Carolina and lose her independence and her identity. But the fact remained that, the longer she stayed here, the harder it was to ignore what they'd once had.

She was so busy trying not to be impressed that when Cole halted outside a larger building than the rest she almost ran into him. 'What do you think?' he asked, and for once his voice was totally devoid of expression.

Joanna frowned, but her attention was caught by the square wooden sign, standing in front of the building. 'The Nathan Smith Clinic,' she read, her breath catching in her throat. 'Oh, God, Cole, did you do this?'

'No.' Cole lifted his shoulders. 'Pa did.' He tied the horses' reins to the rail and went up the steps. 'Come on,' he added flatly. 'I'll show you around. After all, it was your idea originally. No one else cared enough to give a damn.'

The tide was out as they walked the horses along the edge of the water. Joanna had taken off her boots and tied them to the pommel of her saddle, and her toes curled coolly into the damp sand. They had left the estuary and the mud-flats behind, climbing into the dunes to clear the headland, and then dropping down on to the beach again to walk along the shoreline.

Cole hadn't said anything since they left the clinic, and Joanna was finding it difficult to assimilate what she had seen with the man she knew Ryan Macallister to be. He must be pretty desperate to gain Cole's approval, she thought, glancing sideways at the man beside her. She just wished she knew what Cole was thinking, and whether Nathan's death was the only reason he was alienated from his father.

Kicking up a spray of salt water, Joanna tilted her head to look at the sun. Even though it was still early, it burned down hotly on her shoulders—and on her uncovered head. But she refused to wear that hat when she wasn't riding, and she had found some pins and skewered her hair on top of her head.

'What're you thinking?' she asked at last, noticing that the cuffs of her shorts were splashed with sea water. 'I've said I'm impressed. Your father must have had some change of heart.'

'Yeah.' Cole's mouth flattened. 'As soon as he knew his tab was almost up.'

Joanna frowned. 'That's pretty harsh, isn't it?' she murmured. She was no friend of Ryan Macallister's, but she was being compelled to find reasons to be charitable.

Cole slanted a narrow gaze down at her. 'Hey, don't tell me he's getting to you,' he mocked, though there was a dark glint in his eyes. 'Be careful, Jo. You might be tempted to tell me why he wanted you brought here. Or shall I tell you? The old devil's found out he's not immortal, after all.'

Joanna let go of the mare's reins, and stopped at the water's edge, scuffing her toes in the water. 'He wants me to—to intercede with you on his behalf,' she said, deciding she wasn't going to gain anything by keeping silent. 'He says—*Ben* says—you and he don't get on like you used to. Do you want to tell me why?'

'No.'

Cole's response was short and succinct, and Joanna sighed. She was going to get nowhere at this rate, and she still hadn't spoken to him about Charley and Billy Fenton.

And, instead of staying with her, Cole had walked on, his broad shoulders and narrow hips arousing an aching sense of denial. She wanted Cole to care what she thought, what she did, Joanna realised painfully. But, however much she might torment him, ultimately, she would be the loser.

'Damn you, wait!' she exclaimed now, stamping her foot, and then made a sound of frustration as the water splashed up to her thighs. She had forgotten where she was for a moment, and now she was nearly soaked to the skin.

Cole had walked a few yards further on but then either a sense of responsibility or simply curiosity caused him to stop and look back. And, acting purely on impulse, Joanna reached down and unfastened her trousers.

That, at least, aroused some reaction. 'Cut it out,' he snapped, striding back to where she was standing, but Joanna only kicked off the cut-offs, and draped them over the saddle.

'They're wet,' she said, shivering in spite of the heat. For, although she was aware that her briefs were no less modest than the bottom half of her bikini, there was something wholly devastating in watching Cole's eyes flick over them.

'This is South Carolina, not the South of France,' he said through gritted teeth, snatching the cut-offs from the saddle, and thrusting them into her hands. 'They'll dry. Put them on.'

'They'll dry much quicker this way,' declared Joanna, tossing them over the saddle again. Then, before he could stop her, she had skipped away into the creaming surf. 'Let's go swimming, hmm? The water's heavenly!'

'Joanna!'

He said her name slowly, and menacingly, but she refused to be daunted. This might be the last time they were alone together, and, however crazy it might be, she wanted him to have something to remember her by.

'Come on,' she said, deliberately unfastening another button on her shirt, so that he could see the dusky hollow of her cleavage. 'Don't be such a spoil-sport, Cole. Where's your sense of adventure? We used to go skinny-dipping in Tahiti, and you weren't so prudish then!'

Cole didn't hesitate. Completely dumbfounding her, he strode into the waves without even bothering to take his boots off. And, because it was the last thing she had expected, he caught her easily. He grasped her elbow, as she turned to flee, and hauled her back into his arms.

She almost overbalanced him, as she thudded against his hard chest, but he spread his legs and saved them both from being submerged. 'No more games, Jo,' he ordered grimly, dragging her back towards the shore, and she kicked her legs in frustration as he waded out on to the sand.

She had soaked him as well as herself now, and, judging by his expression, he didn't find it at all funny. 'You're crazy, do you know that?' he grated, releasing her to examine his wet thighs. 'For God's sake, what are you trying to prove?'

Joanna stared at him, not really knowing the answer herself. All she knew at this moment was that she still wanted him; that, whatever had happened in the past and whatever might happen in the future, her destiny had brought her there, to this spot, right now.

'Cole,' she said helplessly, and something in her voice seemed to strike a chord inside him. He looked at her then—not as he had looked at her before, but with a weary, tormented expression, and her heart wobbled precariously in her chest.

'Well?' he demanded, and she sniffed to hold back the tears of frustration that prickled behind her eyes.

'I'm sorry,' she whispered, not really knowing what she was apologising for. 'I—I didn't mean to make you mad. Honestly.' She stepped forward and bent to brush the pearls of sea water from the legs of his trousers. 'Here; let me help you——'

'*Don't*!'

His denial was strangled, his hand dashing her wrist aside, and knocking her off balance. She tried to save herself, but she couldn't, and, to her ignominy, she stumbled on to her knees at his feet.

'Oh, *God*!' With a muffled curse, Cole came down on his haunches beside her. 'Did I hurt you?' he muttered, gazing down at her bent head, and Joanna's tongue came to circle her lips, and she raised her face to look at him.

'Only my pride,' she murmured ruefully, as a sand-crab, startled by her invasion of its territory, scuttled away across the sand. She shook her head, and sighed as her hair tumbled down about her shoulders. 'I guess you didn't want my help, hmm? I forgot, I'm not supposed to touch you, am I?'

Cole drew a laboured breath. 'I didn't know you wanted to,' he muttered, and she realised that her fall had taken him off guard. He would never have said such a provocative thing to her in the normal course of events, and her breathing quickened automatically at the possibilities it created.

'Oh—I'm sure you did,' she ventured, her own voice not quite steady, and, straightening her back, she lifted one hand to support herself on his knee. Beneath her damp fingers, she felt the instinctive tightening of his bones, and although she wanted to look she kept her eyes on his.

'This is—most—unwise,' he said, and she realised that his momentary loss of control was being checked. Taking another gulp of air, he firmly removed her hand from his leg, but when he would have released her she held on and brought his fingers to her lips.

She was quite prepared for him to snatch his hand away. Cole was a master at controlling his emotions, and consequently she held it tighter than she might have done. But, although his features tensed, and she

saw a pulse palpitating at his jawline, he let her get
away with it, watching as she put out her tongue and
licked the tips of his fingers.

However, when she was reckless enough to allow her
eyes to drop down his chest and over his flat stomach
to the unmistakable rigidity of his groin, his tolerance
snapped.

'For pity's sake, Jo,' he muttered hoarsely, and she
was quite sure he intended to put an end to it there and
then. But, before he could get to his feet, she slung her
arms around him, and he lost his balance and fell back
on to the sand, with her half-naked body on top of
him.

Her own astonishment at her temerity was nothing
compared to his. Cole lay flat on the sand, gazing up
at her with disbelieving eyes, and for a moment she was
too shocked to take advantage of it. But then the
dawning anger in his gaze, and the subsiding hardness
between his legs, warned her that she was in peril of
losing her only chance of redemption. She was only
where she was now because she had taken him un-
awares. Any minute, he was going to remove her by
force.

With a helpless sense of need, she ignored his forbidding expression and covered his lips with hers,
withstanding his instinctive rejection, and pressing her
tongue into his mouth.

There was a heartbeat when she thought she hadn't
succeeded, when Cole's hands gripping her shoulders
seemed in imminent danger of throwing her aside. She
fully expected to end up in a humiliating heap on the
sand, with Cole standing above her, scowling his contempt.

But her legs splayed across his abdomen detected the moment when the danger passed, and his body came alive again. Although he might despise himself for it, he couldn't prevent his instinctive response. His hands still grasped her shoulders, but his grip was gentling, and as she continued to possess his mouth his pulsing arousal throbbed against her thigh.

'God,' he groaned, leaving her in no doubt as to his frustration, but one hand was tangling in her silky hair, and the other rolled her over so that now he was on top of her. Then, with his thumb grazing the sensitive skin inside her lower lip, he forced her lips apart, fastening his mouth to their trembling sweetness, and filling the soft moist cavity with his tongue.

Joanna lost all sense of time and place. She wasn't even aware of the sand in her hair, or the gritty feel of its damp granules against her back. She hardly noticed the incoming tide, as it swirled in the rock-pools around them, or the cool salty rivulets that wet her legs from her heels to the bottom of her panties. All she was aware of was Cole—his hands, his lips, his tongue; and the satisfying weight of his body, as he ground his hips against her.

Her shirt was open and so was his, and the fine hair that lightly filmed his chest teased the taut nipples of her breasts. Far from feeling cool, she was on fire, and the burning need of his erection demanded to be filled. He cupped her breasts, suckling on their sweetness as sanity slipped away, and everywhere he touched her aroused an ache that only he could assuage.

CHAPTER THIRTEEN

JOANNA awoke to the sound of the phone ringing, and
for a few mindless moments she wondered who it was.
Once upon a time, she had answered the phone without thinking, and in that happy state between sleeping
and waking she only resented the sound.

But then, as consciousness took hold of her, and the
full weight of her present situation descended upon her,
she slumped back against her pillows. These days, she
avoided speaking to anyone, and as she knew it was
most probably either Grace or her mother she let the
annoying buzz go on.

It stopped, finally, and she stretched a hand out of
bed, and turned the clock on the bedside table towards
her. It was half-past ten, she decided, or was it half-
past eleven? Either way, what did it matter? She'd got
nothing to get out of bed for.

Her eyes drifted round the bedroom without enthusiasm. It was a pleasant room, overlooking the gardens at the back of the row of houses, and because the
room faced east it caught the morning sun. She remembered how much fun she had had, when she
bought the lease of the apartment, choosing the delicately patterned wallpaper, and hanging it herself. She
had chosen the furniture, too, unaware that when she
haunted the salerooms, and decided on solid Victorian

pieces, she was actually anticipating the kind of furnishings she would find in her husband's home.

Of course, when she and Cole got married, she had wanted to sell the apartment, but Grace had persuaded her against it. 'Property's a good investment,' she had argued, thinking, but not voicing, her fears for Joanna's future. 'Keep it,' she said. 'As a nest-egg, if nothing else.' And Joanna had had cause to be grateful for that shrewd piece of advice.

Not that what had happened three years ago was any comfort to her now, Joanna reflected. She might have listened to Grace then, but she hadn't listened to her more recently. When she had phoned Grace that night from the Bahamas, and told her she was going back to Tidewater, Grace had warned her to be careful. She should have paid attention. She had been vulnerable, after all.

She sighed now and rolled over, burying her face in the pillow, and praying for oblivion. But it didn't come. She was wide awake now and unprotected. She knew from past experience that nothing she could do would close her mind to the painful jabs of rejection.

And yet, remembering that morning on the beach, she wondered if she really wished to change anything. She had known a brief taste of happiness, and surely that was worth something. But if she hadn't let Cole make love to her, she wouldn't be going through this emotional crisis now. And what price his lovemaking, when all he'd wanted was sexual satisfaction?

And that only because she had initiated it, she admitted honestly. If she hadn't thrown herself at him, she might still have saved her pride. As it was, she knew he resented her for seducing his intentions, for making him do something he despised.

But, at the time, she hadn't been thinking about how he might react when his body was sated. And it was certain he hadn't been thinking too rationally either. Hunger; passion; whatever primitive need had been driving him on had temporarily paralysed his reasoning. With the hot sun blazing down, and the white surf breaking around them, he had opened his trousers and buried himself in her eager body, just as he had done that very first time in London. He had taken her, right there on the beach, in plain sight of anyone who cared to look.

Sometimes, she wished they could have drowned at that moment, while she was still able to pretend that Cole cared for her as much as she cared for him. She often wondered what might have happened if Ben hadn't come across them. Might they even have salvaged something from the wreckage of the past?

Whatever, he managed to attract their attention, without undue embarrassment. His strident whistle was sufficient to bring Cole to his senses, and he dragged himself away from her with unflattering speed. But, in one sense, Ben had been too late, Joanna reflected wryly. Too late to prevent Cole from exposing his own weakness.

And he hadn't forgiven her for that. In the hours that followed, when he learned that his father had suffered a stroke and had been rushed into hospital in Beaumaris, he wouldn't allow her to comfort him. Indeed, he would have nothing to do with her, staying close by his mother's side, and acting the dutiful son.

But he was only acting, Joanna had guessed that. Even though she and Cole had drifted apart, she could still feel his sense of betrayal. He hadn't forgiven his father for what had happened to Nathan. There was still that tremendous gulf between them.

And, although all her own senses were screaming for her to leave now, before he could hurt her again, Joanna knew she had to do something. She had given up hoping that any good could come from Ryan's death. It wasn't going to make any difference to her situation. And while she owed the man nothing, and cared little for his sensibilities, she was afraid of what it might do to Cole.

Right now, Cole was sure that what he was doing was right, and as long as his father lay in that semiconscious state, which some stroke victims achieved, he felt he had nothing to blame himself for. His father was still alive, just, and in the back of his mind there must be the thought that there was still time for a reconciliation. But if Ryan died, that chance would be gone, and Joanna knew, from her own experience with Cole, that the memories of what might have been could tear a soul to shreds.

That was why she approached Cole, the evening before she left Tidewater for the last time. She had decided not to stay any longer. What was the point? Cole ignored her. His mother regarded her as an unwelcome intruder. Even Charley was too upset about her father's illness to spend any time with her, and waiting around for Ryan to die seemed unbearably morbid.

Nevertheless, it took all her courage to go looking for Cole after supper that evening. Meals were taken at irregular times at the moment, and it had been no surprise earlier to find she and Ben were the only ones at the table. Not that Ben was particularly chatty either. She guessed he hadn't forgotten what he had seen several days ago on the beach, and, while he might have sympathy for her, he must know how Cole was treating her.

She found Cole in the library, sitting at his father's desk, going over the stacks of bills that still appeared, whatever the circumstances. The management of the plantation was an ongoing thing, and it simply wasn't possible to abandon these mundane tasks.

Joanna paused in the doorway, checking that almost all the buttons of her full-skirted Indian cotton dress were closed. Patterned in shades of green and black, it was the most conservative item in her wardrobe, and she had worn it deliberately, so that he wouldn't think she had anything provocative in mind.

He didn't look up from the desk, even though she was almost sure he must have heard her footsteps, and she had to clear her throat, and say, 'Cole,' before he chose to acknowledge her presence.

He did look up then, and she flinched at the look of loathing in his eyes. If she had had any doubts about his feelings for her, they were extinguished at that moment. He hated her, and it showed. She wanted to turn right around and leave him.

But she didn't. Determination, conscience, remorse, or simply the need to appeal to him one last time, kept her where she was. Cole might hate her, but she loved him, and she couldn't allow his father's death to poison the rest of his life. Not if she could help it.

She moistened her lips. 'Could I talk to you?'

'What about?'

Cole's voice was as chilling as his expression, and Joanna knew a hopeless sense of grief. 'I—just wanted to tell you, I'm leaving tomorrow,' she said, choosing the least controversial thing she could think of, and then caught her breath uneasily, when he lurched abruptly to his feet.

'You're leaving?' If she hadn't been able to see his face, Joanna might have been deceived by his intonation. He actually sounded shocked at the news, and almost disapproving.

'Y-yes,' she added quickly, glancing behind her at the empty hall, before stepping awkwardly into the room. 'I—I can't stay here indefinitely, can I? And you can't pretend you want me to.'

Cole's feature hardened. 'Have I asked you to leave? Has *anyone* asked you to leave?'

'No—but——'

'So this is your decision.'

'If you put it like that.' Joanna lifted her slim shoulders in a dismissive gesture. 'I—I've got to get back to London. The—the exhibition——'

'Oh, yes. The exhibition!' The way Cole repeated her words was harsh with sarcasm. In a disconcerting gesture, he came round the desk and propped himself against the front. 'I'd forgotten what a famous painter we have in our midst. Art before honour, is that what they say?'

'I've never heard it.' Joanna held up her head. 'And it's not like that at all.'

'So how is it?'

Joanna swallowed. 'If—if I was wanted here——'

'Yes?' Cole's brows ascended. 'If you were wanted—what?'

'I'd stay, of course.'

'On sufferance?'

'No, not on sufferance.' Joanna sighed, growing weary of trying to defend herself to someone who was merely tormenting her. 'I'm not wanted here. You know that, and I know that. It's better if I leave. Before—before——'

'Before my father dies, and you might be called upon to show some sympathy,' finished Cole bleakly, and Joanna's shoulders slumped.

'No,' she said, shaking her head. 'That's not what I meant at all. I just—have no place here any longer. And I think it'll be easier for everyone, if I go back to London.'

Cole's face lost all expression. 'Very well. I'll arrange to have Ben drive you into Charleston tomorrow afternoon.'

'Thank you.'

But as Cole pushed himself up from the desk, and started back to his seat, she lingered. She still hadn't said what she'd come here for, and, although the prospect was even more daunting now, she had to try.

'Is there something else?'

Cole had paused beside his desk, and was looking at her with cold, wary eyes, and she shivered. Had she only imagined that morning on the beach? she wondered. She could see little of that man in this remote, unapproachable stranger. Did nothing ever touch him these days? Not even making love . . . ?

Only it hadn't been love, she reminded herself painfully. It had been sex, pure and simple. She had aroused him, and he had responded. At best, they had used each other.

Now Joanna came forward again, until her hands were within reach of the leather-tooled surface of the desk. But she didn't touch it, even though she would have welcomed its support. Her damp fingers were linked tightly together—an indication, if he had needed it, of just how nervous she was.

'It's about your father,' she began, and, ignoring Cole's grim features, she hurried on, 'Can't you forgive him? Oh, I know I've said some harsh things about him in the past, and I know what he did was wrong, but you have to try and forget it. When—when the truth about Nathan came out, he must have panicked. Of course he was angry. Of course he blamed me for making friends with Nathan, and causing it to happen. Maybe he didn't realise how sensitive Nathan was. No one could have guessed what would happen. No one wanted Nathan to die. It was an accident—a horrible accident! It doesn't serve any purpose to crucify the past!'

Cole stared at her impassively, but there was scorn in his voice, as he exclaimed harshly, 'This was what he wanted, wasn't it? This was what he brought you here for? You were meant to plead his case for him. God, I should have guessed!'

Joanna expelled a breath she'd hardly known she was holding, and wondered if Ryan had really thought her appeal would do any good. Cole wouldn't listen to her. He didn't even like her. How could his father imagine that she would stand a chance?

'I'm right, aren't I?' Cole said now, and her silence was answer enough. 'Well, what a pity he left it too late! I guess Nemesis refused to be cheated.'

Joanna sighed. 'It's not too late,' she burst out desperately. 'Not for you, anyway. Make your peace with him, Cole. For your sake, if not for his. Do it, I beg you. If you don't, you're the one who'll regret it. He won't be around to care.'

The silence that greeted this last remark went unbroken. And, for the life of her, Joanna couldn't think of anything else to say. She'd done what she could.

Now it was up to Cole. But, looking at his bleak face, she doubted it had been enough.

She slipped away then, and returned to her room to do her packing. She felt numb—not only because she knew she had lost the only thing that had any real value for her, but also because she had perjured herself for no reason. Cole wouldn't listen to her advice, and how could she blame him? It was difficult to be convincing, when you didn't believe what you were saying.

The next morning, Cole didn't appear at breakfast, and she guessed he was keeping out of the way until she had left. It was obviously easier for him that way, but was it really easier for her? Hadn't she secretly hoped to see him if only to say goodbye?

Maggie came out to the car, as Ben was loading her suitcases. She came round to where Joanna was standing, and, in spite of the fact that she had no reason to resent her any longer, Cole's mother couldn't resist having the final word.

'You're leaving,' she said, and there was a wealth of satisfaction in her words. 'Cole give you your marching orders, did he? I knew he would, sooner or later.'

Joanna swallowed. 'It wasn't like that. I—have to get back to London.'

'Really.' Obviously, Maggie didn't believe her. 'Seems like he can't wait to get shot of you.'

Joanna refused to be provoked. She knew it was what the other woman wanted, and she was determined not to give her that satisfaction as well.

'Well, you're wrong,' she declared pleasantly, wishing Maggie's bulk wasn't preventing her from opening the station-wagon door. 'It was my decision.'

'As it was your decision to try and break up this family, right?' Maggie demanded harshly, giving up all pretence of being civil. 'Cole hasn't forgiven you for that, so don't you forget it!'

Joanna gasped. 'I didn't try to break up your family!'

'Then what would you call it? Believing all those lies about Ryan and that woman! That boy could have been any man's bastard! How do you know he was Ryan's? He didn't even look like him!'

Joanna frowned. 'I didn't even know you'd seen Nathan,' she said, trying to remain calm, and Maggie's plump features reddened.

'Oh, I saw him all right,' she blurted defensively. 'I saw the two of you together lots of times. Down there on the river-bank. I told Cole what you were doing. I told him you couldn't wait to give another man what you were denying your lawful husband!'

Joanna gulped. 'You saw us!' She shook her head. 'Nathan and I were friends!' she protested weakly. 'Just friends!'

'And I bet you think I still believe in the tooth fairy,' Maggie sneered. 'There's no man here gonna believe you didn't let that misbegotten son of a bitch get between your legs, girl! Hell, you were quick enough to believe the worst about Cole's daddy!'

Joanna swayed. For a moment, she was sure she was going to pass out, and a cold sweat broke out on her forehead. Although the day was hot, she felt chilled to the core of her being. Oh, God, she felt so dizzy. She could feel all the blood draining out of her face.

'Hey—don't you go fainting on me, girl!'

Maggie grabbed her arm, and it was a measure of Joanna's weakness that she didn't try to shake her off. 'It's not true,' she whispered, gazing at Cole's mother with wide, accusing eyes. 'I didn't—I wouldn't—I never slept with Nathan. You have to believe me, I've never slept with any man but Cole.'

Maggie bundled her aside, and wrenched open the car door. 'Don't matter none now,' she declared, hustling her into the station wagon, and Joanna realised that Cole's mother didn't believe it herself. She had probably never believed it. But it was a way to poison Cole's mind against her, and she used it. As she would have used anything to destroy their marriage, and everything it represented . . .

CHAPTER FOURTEEN

WHICH was why she felt no will to get out of bed these mornings, Joanna reflected, glancing at the clock without interest. Since she got back to London, she had had no enthusiasm for anything, and her parents weren't the only ones who were anxious about her. Grace was worried, too, particularly as Joanna refused to talk about what had happened at Tidewater. For the first time since they had become friends, there was a barrier between them, and no amount of cajoling on Grace's part could break through the shell she'd erected.

It wasn't that she blamed the other woman for what had happened. Heavens, Grace had warned her about going there, even if she had felt some compassion for Cole's father. But Joanna simply didn't have the heart to tell her what had happened as she was leaving. That was simply too painful to confide to anyone.

And she felt such a fool, too. All these years, she had blamed Cole for using his brother as a scapegoat. She had thought Cole wanted a divorce, and that he had used her friendship with Nathan to achieve his own ends. She had never dreamt his mother might have been lying to him behind her back. No wonder he had reacted so violently, when he found Nathan at the clinic.

And the trouble was, if she permitted thoughts like that to germinate, it put in doubt the whole question of why their marriage had failed. Who knew how long Cole had been fed those lies? Their relationship had been in jeopardy ever since he got back from South America. Might he never have got involved with Sammy-Jean, if he hadn't thought she was having an affair?

It was thoughts like these that she had to keep at bay. And she couldn't do that if she spoke of them to Grace. It had been hard enough remembering what Cole had said to his father the night Nathan died, and realising how easy it had been for her to misinterpret his actions afterwards. But, if she ever allowed Maggie's malicious words to mean anything to her, she might truly lose the will to live altogether.

The phone started to ring again, and Joanna pulled a pillow over her head to drown out the sound. But it didn't go away, not even when she reached out and snatched the receiver off its hook, and buried it beneath the bedcovers. The intrusive, persistent sound went on and on, and she realised it was the visitor's intercom from downstairs.

She contemplated not answering it, but Grace would know she was here. Her curtains were still drawn, for heaven's sake. She wished now she had got up earlier and drawn back the curtains, so that she could at least have pretended to be out. But, even so, Grace was unlikely to believe it. Not since she had refused to attend her own first exhibition.

Pushing herself up, she slid her legs over the side of the bed. But, as she padded wearily towards the door, a wave of nausea hit her. It was so unexpected that she hardly had the time to turn and dash for the bathroom, before she was suddenly and violently sick.

For a few moments, the insistent buzzing from downstairs was drowned out by the heavy thumping of her heart. She leaned over the basin, feeling her stomach churning, and trembling like a jelly. For God's sake, she thought weakly, whatever had she eaten? She couldn't believe the tin of soup she had had for supper the night before was responsible for her feeling so ill.

But, to her relief, the nausea subsided as quickly as it had appeared. By the time she had wiped her face on a towel, and examined her pale features in the mirror, she was feeling almost normal. And the buzzing had stopped, she noted gratefully. Oh, well, if it was Grace, undoubtedly she would come back.

Then, as she turned on the taps in the shower, a shattering thought occurred to her. It was exactly six weeks since she had left Tidewater. Six weeks, and she hadn't had a period in all that time!

Turning off the taps again, and with remarkable calmness, she padded back into the bedroom and pulled her diary out of the bedside drawer. She didn't keep a diary, except as a kind of calendar, and she riffled through the pages, looking for the dates in question.

A few moments later, she dropped the diary back into the drawer, and sank down weakly on to the side of the bed. She was right, she acknowledged, even though the written proof had been incidental. Her body clock was already telling her all she needed to know. She had actually missed her second period, and unless there was something radically wrong with her metabolism—which she doubted—there was every possibility that she was pregnant.

Her breath escaped on a wispy sigh. 'Pregnant!' She said it out loud, as if she needed to hear the word to believe it. She was going to have a baby. After all those barren months, when she had begun to believe she might never get pregnant, the impossible had happened. Cole's baby was already growing inside her.

Then she tried to be rational. She didn't know that for sure, she told herself firmly. Accidents happened. She might just be going through some biological upheaval. It was even possible that her emotional state might have something to do with it.

But, deep inside her, she didn't really believe that. As she ran a tentative hand over her still flat stomach, she felt a growing conviction that the baby was real. She wasn't inventing the way she felt; she hadn't imagined her sickness. That morning, on the beach at Tidewater, Cole had given her more than he could ever have imagined.

Cole...

She licked her dry lips. What was she going to do about Cole? Was she going to tell him, and run the risk of his mother trying to take the baby away from her? But how could she keep it from him? Oh, God! The child was his, too.

And then the doorbell rang. Her doorbell this time. Not the buzzer from downstairs. Evidently Grace had bluffed her way into the building. But how could she talk to her now, when she needed time to consider what she was going to do?

Of course, she didn't have to tell Grace, she acknowledged, getting up from the bed again, and opening the bedroom door. She crossed the hall into the living-room, as the doorbell rang once more, and she grimaced. It wasn't like Grace to be so impatient. She must be really worried this time.

But an innate caution, born of these years of living alone, stopped her from actually opening the door right away. It was always possible that someone else knew she lived alone, and she had no desire to become another statistic on London's list of crimes against women in their own homes.

'Grace?' she called, her hand on the deadlock, ready to release the latch.

'No. It's Cole,' declared a low attractive male voice that she had never expected to hear again. 'Come on, Jo. Open up! I was beginning to think Aunt Grace must be wrong, and you weren't home.'

Joanna slumped against the panels, her fingers falling nervelessly from the bolt. '*Cole*,' she breathed disbelievingly. Dear God, had she conjured him up out of the air? And what was he doing here in London? He couldn't know about the baby. She'd only just discovered that herself!

'Jo, come on.' His voice sounded a little terse now, as if he was afraid she wasn't going to answer, and he was using impatience to hide his uncertainty. 'I'm not going away until I talk to you.'

Joanna took a steadying breath and straightened her spine. 'What about?' she asked, her voice as thin and reedy as her stretched nerves, and, although it was barely audible, she heard the muffled oath he uttered.

'Let me in and I'll tell you,' he stated at last. 'Please, Jo. It's important. I haven't flown all this way just to shout at you through the keyhole.'

Joanna gave a helpless shrug, and looked down at her crumpled nightshirt. 'I—I'm not dressed,' she said, using the only excuse she could think of. But it was a valid one, she thought ruefully. She wouldn't want anyone to see her in this state, least of all *him*.

'God, Jo, I don't care if you're stark naked,' he grated, and she heard his fist thud against the door in frustration. 'This isn't a social visit. I need to talk to you. Now, can you cut the waffle, and open this damn door?'

Joanna's mouth went dry. 'I can't. I'm a mess——'

'I've told you, I don't care what you look like.'

'No, but——'

'*Jo!*'

His use of her name was desperate, and, realising it must be something pretty serious to bring him all this way, Joanna gave in. But she still didn't unlock the door.

'Look,' she called, 'give me a few minutes, will you? I—I'll put something on. Hold on.'

Cole said something else, something not very complimentary, she guessed, but she couldn't help it. He would have to wait until she had had a wash, and changed into something decent. Her pride wouldn't let her face him looking such a hag.

Ten minutes later, with her face washed and her teeth cleaned, and a deliberately chosen georgette tunic, in a becoming shade of apricot, giving warmth to her pale features, Joanna opened the door. Her hair was loose, a dusky fall of silk that swung against her cheek as she stepped back to let him in.

She thought, belatedly, that she should have worn something on her feet. In the ordinary way, Cole towered above her. When she was in her bare feet, he was a force to be reckoned with.

And her instinctive recoil when he stepped into the apartment was as much a reaction to the threat he represented as social politeness. She didn't want him there, not now, not while she was still trying to come to terms with her condition. God, she hadn't even decided what she was going to do about the baby. And she certainly wasn't ready to give him that advantage.

Even so, as he stepped forward and took hold of the door to close it behind his back, she had a moment to study his taut features. Her initial thought that he hadn't changed had to be slightly revised. He had changed. He looked older for one thing. And thinner, too, if she wasn't mistaken. Evidently his father's death—for surely Ryan was dead now, and that was why he was here—had hit him rather harder than he had imagined. She hoped he wasn't blaming himself for what had happened. She hoped he had made his peace with his father, however painful that had proved to be.

She took a nervous breath. It was strange seeing Cole in a suit, for once. It made him look more serious, more severe. The dark grey fabric threw the lightness of his hair into prominence, shadowing his cheek-bones, and accentuating the thin line of his mouth. And it also served to make him look more remote, and more unapproachable. This was not the man who had made such desperate love to her on the beach. This was still the stranger who had faced her in his father's study.

But she hadn't looked into his eyes, and, when she did so, her interpretation had to be revised once again. There was an uneasy tension in his gaze, and raw desperation. No, not the unfeeling stranger, she thought unsteadily, but perhaps an approximation.

Nevertheless, his presence disturbed her. No matter how she tried to rationalise her feelings, just looking at him gave her a shivery feeling in the pit of her stomach. She hoped it wasn't physical. She hoped she wasn't going to throw up again while he was here. It would be too embarrassing if she had to go dashing into the bathroom. And, while he'd never guess the real reason, he might get the wrong impression.

The silence was unnerving, and Joanna was too emotional to cope with it right now. 'I—how are you?' she said, realising how inane that sounded after everything that had gone before, but incapable of thinking of an alternative. 'I—I never expected——'

'Grace said you'd been ill,' he interrupted her abruptly, moving away from the door, so that Joanna felt obliged to back further into the room.

She swallowed. 'Ill?' she said faintly. Was that why he was here? Because Grace had sent for him? 'I—I'm fine, really. I don't know what—what gave her that opinion.'

Cole frowned. 'She said you're not working.'

'Oh, that!' Joanna managed to give a short laugh. 'No—well, I'm not. But I don't think that's any concern of yours.'

Cole's jaw tightened. 'Nevertheless, I am concerned——'

'Well, don't be.' Joanna didn't think she could stand this stilted conversation one minute longer. 'If Grace has taken it upon herself to contact you and blame you, because I'm being lazy, then I'm sorry. You've had a wasted journey. I—I'll work again, when I feel like it.'

'She says you didn't even attend your own exhibition.'

'So what?' Joanna was beginning to resent him and Grace for putting her in this position. It was bad enough feeling as if her life had lost all meaning. The last thing she needed was Cole coming here to offer her some guilty consolation.

'So—she's worried about you,' he said shortly, but she had the feeling that Grace's emotions weren't the whole reason he had come. 'God, Jo, do you have to make this so bloody hard? I really hoped you might be glad to see me.'

Joanna tensed. 'Is that what Grace said?'

'To hell with Grace!' retorted Cole savagely. 'Is that the only reason you can think of why I might be here?'

Comprehension dawned. With an effort, Joanna remembered what she had thought when he first came into the apartment. Of course. He must have come to tell Grace his father was dead. It was the kind of thing he would do. So much more civilised than putting it in a letter.

Now she shook her head. 'I'm sorry.'

Cole closed his eyes for a moment, and then opened them again. 'What are you sorry for now? Not my wasted journey again, I hope.'

'No.' Joanna gave a helpless gesture. 'A-about your father. I—I might not have liked him, but I didn't wish him——'

'Dead?' Cole cut in harshly, and she nodded. 'Well, I'm afraid your condolences are just a tad premature.'

Joanna stared at him. 'You mean——?'

'I mean my father is still very much alive.' Cole loosened the button of his collar and dragged his tie a couple of inches away from his neck, as if he was feeling the heat. 'He's even recovered his powers of speech, although he isn't always intelligible. It rattles him like hell, but he makes himself understood, one way or the other.'

Joanna was astounded. 'Grace never told me.'

'Grace didn't know.' Cole paused. 'Not until an hour ago, anyway. I gather you didn't tell her about his stroke.'

'No.' Joanna was beginning to feel uneasy, and she glanced behind her, as if she was getting bored with the conversation. 'I—I haven't talked to Grace much since I got back. I—I—I've been . . .'

'Too busy?' suggested Cole sardonically, and Joanna felt the warm colour invade her throat.

'Not—exactly,' she said, holding up her head. 'I—do have a life outside of painting.'

'Do you?'

Cole's tone was vaguely accusing, and Joanna wondered what he had expected her to say. For heaven's sake, he knew, better than anyone, how she had felt when she left Tidewater. It wasn't as if he hadn't known she was leaving. Didn't he remember his chilling rebuttal?

Taking a deep breath, she decided this one-sided attack had gone on long enough. 'Why have you come here, Cole?' she asked. 'I'm sure it wasn't to inform me that your father is back at Tidewater——'

'He's not.' Cole broke into her words with a swift denial.

Joanna frowned. 'He's not what?'

'Back at Tidewater.' He paused. 'I said he wasn't dead. I didn't say he was back home.'

'Does it matter?' Joanna felt totally indifferent to his statement. 'As I say, I don't believe your father's— partial recovery was why you came to see me.'

'It wasn't.' Cole took a step forward, and Joanna felt uneasy again. She wasn't ready for this, she thought unsteadily, wishing Grace had warned her that he was coming. But perhaps she had. She remembered those unanswered phone calls with a bitter sense of regret. 'I came because I thought we needed to talk.'

'What about?'

'How about—us?' ventured Cole, with cool audacity. 'Like maybe we're not finished yet. Despite all the signs to the contrary.'

Joanna's arms flailed. 'Grace did send you here, didn't she?' she exclaimed. 'Oh, I wish she'd——'

'Grace didn't even know I was coming to London,' Cole retorted, grasping a protesting arm, and refusing to let go. 'Listen to me, Jo, I'm the last person Aunt Grace would choose to get in touch with. If she's worried about you—and she is—she wouldn't send for the man who she believes is to blame for it all!'

Joanna stared at him indignantly, but his words did have some merit. Grace might love Cole as a nephew, but she had always been wary of him as Joanna's husband. And, knowing what had happened in the past, she was hardly likely to appeal to him now.

His hard fingers were beginning to bite into the soft flesh of her upper arm, and, as if becoming aware of it, Cole uttered an oath and released her. But he didn't move away. He stayed where he was. And she was still overwhelmingly aware of him, and the threat he represented.

'Look,' he said, and when he spoke again the husky timbre of his voice scraped insistently across her nerves. 'I didn't come here to argue with you. God knows, we've done enough of that in the past.'

'I suppose that's my fault!'

Joanna's response was swift and indignant, but it was as much a protest against the unwilling awareness he was arousing as a defensive ploy. It was hard to remain detached, when his warm breath was wafting over her forehead, and the male scent of his sweat was filling her nose.

'No,' Cole retorted now. 'It's mine.' And she was still trying to absorb this when he added, with bitter self-recrimination, 'I shouldn't have believed my mother's lies, but, when you're in love with someone, you're vulnerable!'

Joanna's knees went weak. 'I—beg your pardon?' she whispered, groping behind her for the back of a chair, anything that could give her some support. And Cole moved a little nearer.

'I said, I was—I still am—in love with you. Why did you think my father and I were estranged? He knew damn well there was only ever going to be one woman in my life. And he'd driven you away. He and my mother between them.' His blue eyes darkened with emotion, as he added, 'That's why I'm here, Jo. That's the only reason. I knew I had to try and make you believe it.'

Joanna had never fainted in her life, but for once she felt near to it. Cole's face was wavering before her eyes, and she was fairly sure she must have imagined what she thought he just said. Was this what losing consciousness felt like? she wondered, unaware of just how pale she'd become.

'I—don't feel very well,' she said, feeling foolish, and Cole's ejaculation was harsh and self-derisive.

'Goddammit,' he muttered, abandoning any lingering shred of self-control, and swinging her up into his arms. 'I always was a tactless bastard. I'm sorry. I'd forgotten Grace told me you were sick.'

'I'm not sick,' argued Joanna faintly, as Cole carried her across to her settee, and deposited her on it. 'Really, I'm not. I—guess it's just the heat.'

'Or what I said,' said Cole grimly, dropping his jacket on to a chair, and perching on the edge of the sofa beside her. He tugged off his tie, and sent it curling on to the floor. 'I didn't intend to blurt it out like that, but, hell, I had to get your attention!'

Joanna felt better now that she was off her shaky legs, but the hard strength of the thigh beside her hip was still daunting. And now that he was without his jacket she could see the shadow of brown skin beneath his cream silk shirt, and glimpse the sun-bleached hair that arrowed down his chest.

'It doesn't matter,' she said, wishing she dared ask him to repeat what he had blurted out. 'Um—do you think I could have a drink of water?' she added, desperate to find some way of getting a little breathing space. 'I haven't had anything to eat this morning, and I am feeling a bit empty.'

'You haven't had breakfast?' Cole got to his feet and towered over her, and now her eyes were irresistibly drawn to the narrow cut of his trousers. Was it her imagination, or were they tighter than they should have been across his hips? Dear God, she thought unsteadily, she was rapidly losing control.

Shaking her head in answer to his question, she was unutterably relieved when he strode away into the kitchen. In the few moments it would take him to find a glass, and run the tap, she had to calm herself. And there was no way she could do that if she thought about what he'd said.

The sense of unreality had passed by the time Cole came back, carrying a tray. But it must have taken longer than she'd thought, she reflected ruefully, for he'd taken the time to filter some coffee and make some toast. Of course, he knew his way around her kitchen, she conceded. He had lived here for several weeks before their wedding. Oh, those blissful days, she remembered wistfully. Before the coils of Tidewater had strangled their relationship.

Cole hooked a low coffee-table with his foot, and set the tray down beside the sofa. Then, to her consternation, he resumed his earlier position beside her.

'Coffee, and toast,' he said unnecessarily, his eyes disturbingly warm and intent. 'Can you sit up?'

'I'm not an invalid,' said Joanna, her voice sharper than it might have been because she was nervous, and Cole inclined his head.

'If you say so,' he allowed, respecting her obvious wish to be independent. He let her shuffle into a sitting position, and then reached for the jug of coffee. 'Cream, but no sugar. You see, I remembered that, too.'

Joanna wanted to say something flip and casual, anything to dispel the unwilling intimacy of their situation, but the smell of the coffee was turning her stomach.

'I—think I'd prefer a glass of water, after all,' she declared, struggling to contain her nausea. 'I—excuse me, for a moment. I have to go to the bathroom.'

When she came back, the tray had disappeared, and Cole was standing by the window, staring out on to the sun-baked grass in the park across the way. His hands were in his pockets, but there was tension in every muscle of his taut frame. But he had evidently heard her behind him, because he glanced over his shoulder as she hovered in the doorway, and his mouth flattened ruefully, as he said, 'I guess you want me to go.'

Joanna, who had just spent the last few minutes learning how appalling it was trying to be sick on an empty stomach, hesitated long enough for him to assume she did. With a tightening of his lips, Cole bent to lift his jacket from the chair where he had dropped it earlier, but when he turned towards the door desperation made her reckless.

'I—what you said,' she stammered, hoping she might bluff him into some kind of confession, 'did you—did you mean it?'

Cole's brows drew together. 'I've said a lot of things,' he replied wearily. 'And I'm not proud of a lot of them.'

'No.' Joanna sighed, realising she was not going to get round it that way. 'Just now. When I asked you why you'd come here. You said—at least, I thought you said—you still—loved me——'

'I do.'

There was no mistake this time, and Joanna clutched the frame of the door with sweating hands. But Cole wasn't rushing towards her with declarations of his intent. He was simply standing looking at her, with a definite air of defeat.

Wetting her dry lips, she tried again. 'But—when I came to see you, the night before I left Tidewater——'

'I was a bastard, I know.' Cole lifted his shoulders in a heavy gesture. 'I guess I was still despising myself for wanting you. And when you said you were leaving, I tried to hurt you as you were hurting me.'

Joanna caught her breath. 'You succeeded.'

'Yes, I know.'

'Then why——?'

'Why did I change my mind?' Cole's lips twisted. 'I'd like to say it was only because I'd begun to suspect that there had been nothing going on between you and Nathan.'

Joanna stared at him. 'There wasn't!'

'No. Well, as I say, I had begun to have my doubts. God, I even had doubts before you walked out on our marriage. But you didn't want to listen to them then. You were too busy hating me for what happened to Nathan.'

Joanna bent her head. 'We all make mistakes. And I didn't hate you. I—just thought I did.'

'Yeah, well—you were pretty damn convincing.' Cole's shoulders hunched. 'And, goddammit, I should have had faith in you. But when you left, I guess I convinced myself that you must be guilty.'

Joanna swallowed. 'So what did change your mind?'

'Ben.'

'Ben?'

'Yes. He heard what Ma said to you as you were leaving. How she'd seen you with Nathan, and spread those lies about you.'

Joanna stiffened. 'She never said they were lies,' she stated honestly. 'As far as I know, she believed that Nathan and I—that we were——' She broke off unsteadily. 'If Ben told you she admitted making the whole thing up, he wasn't telling the truth either.'

She waited then for Cole's expression to change. She hadn't really believed that their problems could be solved so easily, and learning what had brought him here only reinforced that fact. It had been kind of Ben to tell him, kind of him to lie, if that's what he had done. It proved she had at least one friend at Tidewater. At least one member of Cole's family wanted to make amends.

But Cole's expression didn't change, except perhaps to grow a little gentler. 'I know exactly what she said,' he told her. 'Ben gave me it, word for word. But what you don't know is that I never knew until then who it was feeding me that information. Ma didn't talk to me, Jo. She sent me letters, anonymous letters. They started right after I got back from South America. So far as I knew, Ma didn't even know of Nathan's existence.'

Joanna's jaw sagged. 'But how do you know your mother was sending those letters?'

Cole's face hardened. 'I confronted her with it after you'd left, and she had the nerve to tell me she'd done it for my own good.'

'For your own good?'

'Yes. It turns out Ma knew all about my father's involvement with Sarah, and about Nathan, too. But there was nothing she could do about it, not without incurring my father's wrath, so she kept it all bottled up inside her. Then, when you and Nathan got to know one another, she saw a chance to—to——'

'Kill two birds with one stone,' said Joanna shakily. 'Oh, God, Cole! How could she? What had Nathan ever done to her?'

'He existed,' said Cole simply. 'I didn't realise how badly it had affected her until six weeks ago.'

Joanna felt dazed. 'It's unbelievable.'

'I know.'

'Poor Nathan.'

'Yes, poor Nathan.' Cole's mouth tightened. 'Can you ever forgive me?'

'Forgive you?' Joanna realised she was repeating his words, but she couldn't help it.

'Yes, forgive me,' said Cole harshly. 'If I hadn't been so quick to believe the worst of you, none of this need have happened.'

Joanna hesitated. 'And—and Sammy-Jean?'

'What about Sammy-Jean?'

'You—you married her.'

'Yes, I married her.' Cole's shoulders slumped. 'And I know that condemns me in your eyes, doesn't it? But, when you walked out, three years ago, I didn't care what I did any more. It was what Ma wanted,' he added bitterly. 'And, after what Pa had put her through, I thought she deserved a break.'

Joanna trembled. 'Did you love her?'

'If I'd loved Sammy-Jean, I'd have married her five years ago, instead of you,' he replied quietly.

'Oh, Cole!' Joanna moved her head in a helpless gesture, wishing he would put down his jacket and do something, instead of just standing there, staring at her. 'So—what are you saying?'

'I'd have thought that was obvious,' replied Cole flatly, and there was a look of weary acceptance in his eyes. 'I wanted us to be together again. But—I guess I waited too long to tell you.'

CHAPTER FIFTEEN

COLE was turning away, threading his finger through
the tab of his jacket, ready to loop it over his shoulder, when Joanna came to her senses. Abandoning the
unnatural detachment with which she had listened to
his explanations, she flew across the room, and flung
herself into his arms. 'What took you so long?' she
choked, burying her hot face against his chest. 'Oh,
God, Cole, I've missed you so much!'

His reactions were less dramatic than hers, but far
more violent. With a groan of anguish, his arms closed
about her, and she felt his muscles trembling as he
hugged her tight against him.

'I wanted to come after you right away,' he told her
unsteadily, his lips against her ear. 'But there were
things to do, things I had to see to. I wanted you to
know what I was offering, before you made up your
mind.'

Joanna wound her arms about his neck. 'Nothing's
more important than our being together,' she whispered unsteadily. 'And—and as long as you love me,
that's all that matters.'

'No.' Joanna looked a little anxious at his denial, but
Cole pushed his fingers into the silky length of her hair,
and held her face up to his. 'No, that's not all that
matters,' he told her huskily. 'I thought it was once. I
thought where we lived wasn't important. I was so
selfish—so *jealous* of your work—I wanted to absorb

you into my life so completely, you wouldn't have time for anything else.'

'Cole——'.

'No, listen to me,' he implored her. 'I was wrong. I was wrong to expect you to live with my family, and I was wrong to try and stop you from continuing with your career.' His thumb brushed an errant tear from her cheek. 'That won't happen again.'

'Oh, Cole——'

'There's more.' He couldn't resist brushing her soft mouth with his, but when she would have deepened the kiss he drew back. 'If you don't want to go back to Tidewater, we needn't. I'll sell the place if you want, and move to England. It's up to you——'

Joanna gasped. 'You'd *sell* Tidewater? But what about your father and mother?'

'Since Pa had his stroke, I've been given his power of attorney. Besides, Pa will never go back to Tidewater, he knows that. He's been moved to a nursing facility in Charleston, where they can monitor his condition on a day-to-day basis. And Ma? Well, she and Sandy and the twins are staying with Joe and Alicia for the time being. She knew she and I couldn't go on living in the same house, and I guess, eventually, she'll get a place in Beaumaris.'

Joanna stared at him. 'So there's no one living at the house?'

'Only Ben.' Cole grimaced. 'And the staff, of course. Not forgetting Henry.'

'And—that's why you waited this long before you came to see me?'

'Yes.' Cole looked rueful. 'I wanted there to be no more misunderstandings. If—if you agree to marry me again, it'll be on your terms, not mine. I'm not much good at relationships. I always screw up.'

Joanna's lips quivered. 'I wouldn't say that.'

'I would.' Cole drew her even closer, and she revelled in the solid feel of his hard body. 'I've had plenty of time to think, and I don't care about anything so long as we're together. You're all that matters to me. You always were; you always will be.'

Some time later, Cole stepped into the shower cubicle beside her, and Joanna gulped as his damp hands curved possessively about her thighs. Drawing her back against his hips, he took over the task of soaping her breasts and stomach, and Joanna shivered uncontrollably.

They had just spent the last couple of hours renewing their marriage vows in the most satisfying way possible, and it was amazing to feel the stirring heaviness of his arousal against her bottom. 'You're insatiable, do you know that?' she whispered unevenly, as his hands slid down between her legs, and Cole chuckled as he turned her towards him.

'Only where you're concerned,' he assured her huskily. 'Does it bother you?'

'Should it?'

'Only if you're thinking of leaving me again.'

Joanna's smile was gratifying. 'I'm not.'

'Honestly?'

She wound her arms around his neck, and lifted one leg to coil it about him. 'What do you think?'

Cole groaned. 'I think if we don't get out of here pretty soon, I'm going to explode,' he muttered thickly. 'God, Jo, you have no idea what you do to me.'

'I have a pretty good idea,' she giggled softly, as he stepped out of the shower with her in his arms, and grabbed a towel on his way back to the bedroom. 'Hey, you forgot to turn off the taps.'

'To hell with the taps,' retorted Cole tersely, and her laughter died beneath the hungry possession of his mouth.

It was hunger of a different kind that eventually drove Joanna to wriggle away from Cole's sleeping form, and slip her arms into the sleeves of her silk wrapper. For the first time since she got back to England, she felt really hungry, and she was munching her way through a dish of cornflakes when Cole appeared in the kitchen doorway. Unlike her, he didn't have a dressing-gown to wear, and his suit trousers had evidently been pulled on in some haste.

'What's going on?' he asked, eyeing the milky cereal. 'Isn't it a little late for breakfast? I was going to suggest taking you out for lunch.'

'Mmm, that sounds interesting.' Joanna nodded, swallowing another mouthful of the cornflakes. 'When I've finished this I'll get ready.'

'When you've finished that, you won't be hungry,' retorted Cole drily, running an exploring hand over the cloud of fine hair that roughened the brown skin of his chest. 'Don't you have anything else we could eat?'

'Not really.' Joanna was rueful. 'I—I haven't felt much like eating since I got back.'

Cole's eyes darkened at her words, and his mouth took on a decidedly sensual slant. 'I'm sorry, baby,' he said, and it took all Joanna's determination to stop her from getting up and going to him.

'Yes—well, we should talk,' she said, pushing the almost empty dish aside, and Cole frowned.

'I thought we had.'

'Oh—well, yes. We have, of course.' Joanna licked a drop of milk from her lips in unknowing provocation. 'But—there's something else——'

'If it's about Sammy-Jean——'

'It's not.'

'You have to understand, I was sick with jealousy——'

'Cole, it's nothing to do with Sammy-Jean.'

'Charley, then.' Cole moved agitatedly about the kitchen. 'I know what you're going to say, but she's too young to make that kind of a commitment.'

Joanna looked puzzled now. 'What kind of a commitment?'

'With Billy Fenton. You do know about her and Billy Fenton, don't you? She said you did.'

'Oh——' Joanna knew a moment's remorse. 'She told you.'

'No, Ma did,' said Cole flatly. 'And, I have to say, I was probably more inclined to take Charley's side, because of what happened to us.'

'And?' Joanna was nervously aware that she was prolonging the moment when she would have to tell Cole her suspicions about the baby.

'And I've agreed to let her go on seeing him, but she has to go to college. I don't want her doing anything she's going to regret later.'

Joanna looked up at him. 'As you did?'

'Yes. As I did,' said Cole roughly. 'God, Joanna, what is it? What's wrong? There's something, I know——' He broke off. 'I've told you—I'll do anything you say.'

'It's not that.' Joanna hesitated only a moment, and then she got to her feet. 'I don't mind if we live at Tidewater.'

'Are you sure?'

'Yes. I'm sure.' Joanna linked her hands together. 'In fact, I think it's only right that our—our children should be brought up there. It's their heritage. It's where they belong.'

Cole's face cleared. 'Children,' he said wryly. 'You're sure we'll have children, then?'

Joanna nodded. 'I'm sure.'

'Well . . .' Cole came across the room and pulled her into his arms '. . . just for the record, whether we do or we don't, I'd like to say, here and now, you'll always be the most important thing in my life. And——' he took a breath '—if you don't want a family, I can live with it.'

Joanna sniffed. 'You still think I was using some kind of contraception, don't you?'

'No.' Cole shook his head. 'Not any more. Not after everything that's happened. But—maybe we weren't meant to have any children. God, we've got so much! Why should we be greedy and want more?'

Joanna sniffed again. 'But if—if we did have a baby, you wouldn't object?'

'Object?' Cole pulled a long face. 'Why would I object? All I'm saying is, so long as I have you——'

'I think I'm pregnant!'

The words just flipped from Joanna's tongue, but she couldn't stand the suspense any longer, and she watched Cole's face change from gentle reassurance to stunned incredulity.

'Say—what?' he got out jerkily, and Joanna cupped his face between her hands, and ran the pads of her thumbs over his roughening jawline.

'I think I'm pregnant,' she said again, trembling in spite of herself. 'I know it's sudden, but that—that's why I was so ill earlier. It's just the usual morning sickness. I'm pretty sure I'm right.'

Cole's stunned expression was giving way to anxious concern now. 'Have—have you seen a doctor?' he asked, his lips turning against her palm, and she shook her head.

'I just—realised myself, this morning,' she admitted unevenly. 'About five minutes before you rang the bell, to be exact.'

Cole stared at her. 'And you let me——' He broke off, his lean face reddening. 'God, Jo, you should have told me.'

'Would that have stopped you?' she teased, reaching up to brush his mouth with her tongue.

'I—maybe,' he muttered, still not capable of coping with the situation. 'Oh, Jo——'

'You're pleased?'

'I'm pleased.' Cole shook his head. 'It must have been——'

'That morning on the beach,' agreed Joanna huskily. 'I'm so glad I made you do it.'

'Made me?' Cole groaned. 'I don't know how I kept my hands off you as long as I did. From the minute I walked across that patio in Nassau, I knew I was lost.'

'Did you?' Joanna was eager for more. 'Tell me.'

'Well . . .' Cole parted his legs, so that he could hold her more closely against him. 'I didn't want to admit it, but you must have known.'

'No.' Joanna shook her head now.

'Not even that night, in the back of the taxi?' suggested Cole drily. 'Come on, Jo, you knew what happened there. Why'd you think I was so bloody to you afterwards?'

Joanna dimpled. 'I thought that was your usual way—with me.'

Cole laughed too now, softly, and somewhat disbelievingly. 'Oh, Jo, do you have any idea how much I love you?'

'About as much as I love you, I suppose,' she whispered, but he wouldn't have it.

'At least twice as much as that,' he assured her, burying his hot face in her neck. 'And to think my mother almost destroyed us. I'll never forgive her for that.'

Joanna hugged him close. 'I must admit, I blamed your father,' she said. 'But, as it happens, he was responsible for bringing us together again, wasn't he?'

'I doubt if that was his intention,' said Cole ruefully. 'Though, who knows? After he realised Sammy-Jean and I weren't going to make it, he had to abandon his ideas of expanding Tidewater.'

Joanna drew back to look at him. 'I'm so glad you and Sammy-Jean didn't have a baby,' she whispered, and Cole sighed.

'Believe it or not, but I didn't sleep with Sammy-Jean until after you left Tidewater. And then—well, I guess you could say it was a kind of defence. When you sued for divorce——'

Joanna spread her fingers over his lips. 'It doesn't matter.' She managed a misty smile. 'But you are pleased—about the baby, I mean?'

'As long as you are,' he told her gently. 'I meant it about your work. I promise not to stand in your way.'

'Hey——' Joanna allowed a husky chuckle to escape her. 'I'm no great artist, you know. I enjoy sketching and painting. It gives me pleasure. And it's a great way to earn a living. But it's not the most important thing in my life. It never was.'

'Nevertheless——'

'Nevertheless, nothing. The way I feel right now, I don't care if I never see another paintbrush. I'm going to have a baby; *your* baby. Here. Touch me! I want us to share every minute of this miracle!'

It was another hot day at Tidewater, but Joanna was used to the heat by now. It was two years since she and

Cole had got married for the second time, and she no longer wilted every time the temperature climbed into the nineties and above. Besides, she was too busy to notice what was going on with the weather. She was expecting visitors—Grace and Ray Marsden were coming to spend a few days of their belated honeymoon at Tidewater—and with an eighteen-month-old toddler underfoot, and another baby on the way, she had far too much to think about.

But she was looking forward to seeing Grace again. Although her parents had come out for a visit the year before, and she was at last on speaking terms with her mother-in-law, it would be nice to see her old friend and colleague.

She guessed Grace would be agitating about the new series of paintings she was engaged on, but her work was no longer the pivotal part of her life it had once been. Cole, and baby Nathan, had first call on her affections, and she had never felt so fulfilled in her life.

Of course, it hadn't been so easy at first. In those early days, it had been hard to come back to Tidewater as its mistress, and even harder to face those members of Cole's family who had done so much to make their lives intolerable.

But time was an amazing healer, and, although she and his father had never actually become friends, they had achieved a grudging understanding before Ryan died.

Cole's mother had been a different story. Maggie had taken a long time to accept that Joanna was back at Tidewater to stay. But the baby had gone a long way towards effecting a change in her attitude—even if Joanna's and Cole's insistence in calling him Nathan had caused a minor upheaval.

But that was all some time ago now, and, although Joanna knew Maggie had no conscience about what she had done, when it came to choosing between losing a son or gaining a daughter-in-law—even one she didn't like—it was no contest.

It had been a great thrill for Sarah, too, when they named the baby after her son. It hadn't taken Joanna long to realise that, far from not wanting to see Joanna again, Sarah was desperate to talk to someone who had been on such close terms with her son. Of course, Cole had done what he could to make her life easier, and Joanna hadn't been at all surprised to learn that her husband had helped Sarah open her guest house. He had been one of her first visitors, in the weeks before his mother had left Tidewater for good.

For the rest, the twins had never really been involved in their parents' affairs, and Sandy had been too young to understand. Even Joe's wife, Alicia, had unbent sufficiently to offer advice about feeding the baby, and so on. Because her baby had been born a few months before Joanna's, she tended to patronise her younger sister-in-law.

And Joanna let her. It wasn't important, after all. So long as she had Cole, she was content. And making him happy was all she had ever wanted after all.

Cole came in at that moment, and found his wife arranging flowers in the guest bedroom. Her face was flushed, damp strands of night-dark hair were clinging to her cheek, and already the evidence of her five months of pregnancy were beginning to show.

'Hey,' he said, putting his arms around her from behind, and pulling her back against him, 'don't you go overdoing it now. This isn't the first time Grace has visited Tidewater, you know. Remember, she used to live on the plantation.'

'I know.' Joanna had renewed her acquaintance with Grace's ex-husband and her two sons soon after she returned to Tidewater. 'But I want everything to look nice. I wasn't here the last time she came.'

'Well, I want you to take it easy,' declared Cole, turning her round to face him. 'You should be doing nothing more strenuous than sitting at your easel.' His hand caressed the gentle mound of her stomach. 'We don't want Nathan's brother or sister to get upset, do we?'

'Nathan's brother or sister is doing just fine, thank you,' retorted Joanna, covering his hands with her own. 'So—what are you doing back at this time of day? I thought you and Ben were going to Charleston.'

'We did. And—we got the pony for Nathan, just as we promised. Do you want to come and see it? Or haven't you got time?'

Joanna smiled. 'I've always got time for you, darlin',' she teased, and when Cole leant forward to brush her mouth with his lips she deliberately deepened the kiss. 'But—have you got time for me?' she whispered, her fingers moving down to his belt. 'Nathan's taking his nap. So I've got all the time in the world.'

Cole groaned, deep in his throat. 'Jo, how did I survive three whole years without you?'

'I don't know,' she responded huskily. 'But as you've mentioned it, we do have a lot of time to make up...'

MEN MADE IN AMERICA

Fifty red-blooded, white-hot, true-blue hunks
from every State in the Union!

Look for MEN MADE IN AMERICA! Written by some
of our most poplar authors, these stories feature fifty of
the strongest, sexiest men, each from a different state in
the union!

Two titles available every other month at your favorite
retail outlet.

In November, look for:

STRAIGHT FROM THE HEART by Barbara Delinsky
(Connecticut)
AUTHOR'S CHOICE by Elizabeth August (Delaware)

In January, look for:

DREAM COME TRUE by Ann Major (Florida)
WAY OF THE WILLOW by Linda Shaw (Georgia)

You won't be able to resist MEN MADE IN AMERICA!

Relive the romance...
Harlequin®is proud to bring you

A new collection of three complete novels every month. By the most requested authors, featuring the most requested themes.

Available in October:

DREAMSCAPE

They're falling under a spell!
But is it love—or magic?

Three complete novels in one special collection:

GHOST OF A CHANCE by Jayne Ann Krentz
BEWITCHING HOUR by Anne Stuart
REMEMBER ME by Bobby Hutchinson

Available wherever Harlequin books are sold.

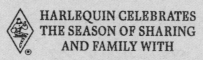